WORDS ON CANDY HEARTS

Augusta Reilly

Published by Rhapsodic Press

Book Cover Design by ebooklaunch.com

To Jeff, who makes all things possible

CHAPTER 1

CLARA

"Loves fades, and sex gets old," Mom said as she took a sip of her gin and bitters. "But money lasts forever."

You've only just met my mom, yet you already understand why every story I tell about my childhood begins with the words *I swear to God I'm not making this up*.

My brain tried to forge a passage through the vodka and find a dry spot where it could do things like think and remember and see straight. But it was no use. I could hold my liquor about as well as I could hold on to a man, and thus it was that after four vodka cranberries at Mom's favorite watering hole on East 63rd Street, I was completely plastered.

With great effort, I lifted my sticky cheek off the bar counter. "You're saying I should become a gold digger?"

"No," Mom said, signaling to her favorite bartender to bring her another drink. "I'm saying that there are qualities a smart girl looks for in a husband and poverty isn't one of them. If you're hell-bent on continuing this PhD thing and becoming a bird doctor—"

"Ornithologist."

"—and insist on spending half your life volunteering for Eco-Justice, you need to find a viable secondary source of income. Your worthless failure of an ex-fiancé certainly wasn't it."

I wasn't sure which was more offensive, my mother referring to Tyler as a "worthless failure" or to the holy institute of marriage as "a viable secondary source of income."

"I loved Tyler for Tyler," I said. "I didn't care about his money."

"How could you?" Mom said. "There wasn't any money to care about."

"He was only two years out of law school. He just needed more time to establish himself." I felt a pounding in my forehead. The vodka was starting to sink in. Deep.

"Why are you still defending that prick?" Mom said, slamming down her glass. "Do I need to remind you what the day after tomorrow is?"

"Please don't."

"It's the day of your cancelled wedding, Clara. The one that sonofabitch called off over fifteen extra pounds. *Fifteen.* Your education and intelligence didn't mean anything to him."

I gestured to the ridiculous getup I was wearing: a skintight miniskirt, equally skintight red blouse with a neckline down to my chest cavity, five-inch heels, and a pair of black fishnet stockings. All loaners from my mom. "If you want me to find a man who respects my intelligence," I said, forcing myself upright, "why did you pick this outfit for me?"

Mom's original plan for our girls' night had been to stay in and watch anything that involved male Marvel characters. But when I arrived at her house in Jersey, she suggested that we drive to the city and find ourselves some real men instead. But I'd come straight from a conservation rally in Ocean County and was wearing a T-shirt that said "I Love Piping Plovers" across the chest. Mom thought "piping plovers" sounded more like a reference to butt sex than a threatened bird species and was worried it would attract the wrong kind of guy. So she lent me some clothes that would attract the right kind of guy, i.e., the kind who liked his women drunk, stupid, and wearing blouses that showcased their underboobs.

"Who said anything about finding a man who respects your intelligence?" Mom said. "I lent you that outfit to help you get laid quick." She took my face in her hands, holding my drunken head so that I could look her three faces in their six eyes. "I'm going to say something, Clara. And I need you to listen carefully, because I'm only going to say this once."

She was about to say, *You're a beautiful woman. And when a man looks at a beautiful woman, he sees one thing and one thing only. A trophy.*

"You're a beautiful woman," Mom said. "And when a man looks at a beautiful woman, he sees one thing and one thing only. A trophy."

"I know," I said. "I remember from the last hundred times you only said it once."

"I wasn't finished yet, wiseass," Mom said. "My point is that once a man sees that gorgeous face of yours, he's never going to see past it to that brain of yours. And once he sees those fabulous tits of yours, he's never even going to try to see past them to that heart of yours."

She let go of my head, and it flopped back onto the bar.

"That's the most depressing thing I've ever heard," I said.

"I'm sorry that reality is depressing," Mom said, returning to her drink. "But the cold hard truth is that there are two kinds of men in this world. Rich bastards and poor bastards. One of them can pay you fifty thousand a month in alimony and the other can give you the five dollars in spare change he found under the couch cushions. Neither will give a shit about your brains or your personality, so you may as well go for the one with the money."

If I actually thought there was any real chance of finding a man who would someday pay me over half a million dollars a year in alimony, I might take Mom's advice and start searching for Mr. Wrong. It had certainly worked out well for her. A former lingerie model, she could wrap any guy around her finger by batting an eyelash. Her last divorce had been years ago, but she was still bringing in twenty thousand a month in alimony. Those funds, combined with her ample freelance earnings, afforded her an extremely comfortable lifestyle.

But I wasn't my mom. And I didn't want to be. Don't get me wrong, I loved her to smithereens, and in her own unorthodox way, she was a great mother. I would go so far as to say that we were best friends. We talked almost every day on the phone, got together in person at least once a week, and vacationed together twice a year. We couldn't get enough of each other, but we bickered constantly and didn't see eye to eye on anything. Particularly men.

Besides, even if I were willing to sell myself out as a trophy wife, there weren't nearly as many millionaires and billionaires out there as popular fiction would have you believe. And who the hell were all these women looking at Bill Gates and Warren Buffett and saying, *I gotta score me a piece of that?* Real billionaires weren't hot. Real billionaires weren't sexy. And real women didn't just bump into them walking down the street.

"Can I please go home now?" I said. *Can I pleath go home now?*

"You've barely started slurring," Mom said. "The fun's just starting. You want to leave already?"

"Yeth."

"You can go home if you want to," she said. "I'm just getting started."

We stood up and gave each other a hug. "Thanks for keeping me company tonight, Mom."

"No problem," she said, squeezing me tight. "And no driving. Leave your car in the street and pick it up tomorrow. Do you need money for a cab?"

"I'm good," I said. "Love you, Mom."

She popped a quick kiss on my cheek. "Love you, too, princess."

I stumbled out onto the street. My forty-nine-year-old mother's night was "just getting started," but at ten p.m., it was a half hour past my twenty-eight-year-old bedtime. All I wanted was to find my car, lock the doors, and sleep it off. With any luck, I'd be sobered up and driving home to Morningside Heights before sunrise.

Somewhere in New York City, a car was parked. It was blue, it was shorter than I was, and it had the letters C and Z on it somewhere, presumably the license plate.

I walked up the block, then back down again, looking for the letters C and Z, but couldn't find them anywhere. It was as I was making my way up the block for the third time that I realized something. CZ were my initials. Clara Zapata. I was so goddammed drunk that I was confusing myself with my license plate. Thank God for sudden moments of clarity.

Ha. Clarity. Get it? Clara-ty. I had a moment of clara-ty.

Ha. Ha ha ha ha.

CHAPTER 2

IAN

"Boob job," I said.

The topic at hand was the extremely well-endowed redhead sitting at the other side of the bar and unabashedly giving me the eye.

"And that's a problem because . . .?" My dad left his question hanging. He was of the mindset that all boobs were good boobs. Big or small, real or fake—it didn't matter. Nor did it matter to whom they were attached. Or if they were even attached. I swear to God, if my womanizing father walked into a plastic surgeon's office and saw a D-cup saline implant in a Petri dish, he'd name it Amber and ask it out on a date.

"It's a problem because fake boobs mean she's shallow, Dad."

"And that's a problem because . . .?" he repeated.

"Because some of us prefer a woman with a personality to a woman stuffed with silicon."

Dad just looked at me, his expression blank.

"A personality's this thing where a woman says interesting things and does interesting stuff," I explained. "It's a byproduct of having a brain."

"I know what a personality is," Dad said. "I just don't understand why it's so important to you."

"Did it ever occur to you that if you married a woman for her personality instead of her appearance, you might not be paying two million dollars a month in alimony?"

"In case you haven't been counting, I've been married five times," Dad said. "That makes me an expert on marriage. Trust me, no matter how intelligent or interesting a woman is, you run out of things to talk about. You get tired of doing the same old stuff over and over again. But a thing of beauty," he continued, raising his glass in toast to titties everywhere, "is a joy forever. Especially if you know a good plastic surgeon."

"That's beautiful, Dad," I said, taking a sip of my ginger ale. "You should have it engraved on your Rolex."

Every time I got together for a drink with my father, I remembered why I did everything in my power to avoid getting together for a drink with my father. People were ornaments to him. He had a lawyer for every day of the week, not because he needed them, but because he thought reigning over a fistful of lawyers meant he was a man of stature. He had fifteen live-in servants across his six houses (including one he'd never stepped foot in), because what billionaire in his right mind didn't want legions of servants scampering around his manifold mansions saying, *Yes, sir, right away, sir?* And women? They were the most prized ornament of all, the cherry atop the Daniel Dunning cupcake.

But I had no choice but to conspicuously spend time with him. I was his only son and thereby an inextricable part of the never-ending PR campaign that was his life.

After several personal disgraces early in his career—including being a famously shitty father—he'd needed to reinvent himself as a decent human being. So at least once a month, his secretary arranged for us to spend "quality time" together in a public venue so the whole world could see what a loving and supportive relationship he had with his only son.

"Smile," Dad said. "People are looking."

I smiled. "Thanks for finding me a fabulous set of boobs to love, Pops, but I think I'll stick to personality."

He took a sip of his tequila. "Greta had a personality. And look what happened."

I said nothing, thinking of the woman who, eight months after our breakup, I still couldn't quite let go. Greta Ann Granger. The initials alone should have told me what I was getting myself into. But I never saw it coming. All I saw was sheer perfection. I met her three years earlier at a fundraiser gala sponsored by our family's charitable foundation. The cause at hand was special education, and Greta was a teacher at one of the city's many underfunded schools. She gave the most beautiful speech I'd ever heard. She was smart, funny, educated, and she was absolutely devoted to the special-needs children in her care. By the end of the evening, I had pledged five million dollars from the Dunning Family Charitable Trust.

And I had fallen madly in like. After filling out my pledge paperwork, I asked Greta to join me for a drink, and we ended up talking until the wee hours of the morning. I couldn't believe how much we had in common. We both loved the seaside on fall days. We both hated crowds and preferred the company of one good friend to a gala full of partygoers. We both wanted kids but were worried about the world we'd have to raise them in. The list went on and on. Two years later, I was down on one knee, and she was answering "Yes" before I'd even finished saying "Will you."

And then I did the dumbest thing I'd ever done in my life: I followed my father's advice and asked Greta to sign a prenup.

She was gone before I woke up the next day. I spent the next five months in a state of constant regret, telling myself Greta had left because I'd hurt her, because I'd suggested her love for me wasn't genuine. Because while she'd been on the phone all day with caterers and florists and banquet halls planning for the wedding, I'd been on the phone all day with lawyers and estate managers planning for the divorce.

For months, I wished I could turn back the clock and undo the damage I'd done by asking for that stupid prenup. But then I heard she was engaged again, and her new fiancé was Lincoln Reynolds, the one and only unmarried son in Manhattan who stood to inherit more money than me. It was when I heard the details of their "chance" meeting that I realized what a fool I'd been. Wouldn't you know it, Greta met Lincoln at a fundraiser gala. Turned out she went to lots and lots of fundraisers. Because you know who you find by the yachtload at gala fundraisers? Millionaires. Billionaires. And their single, eligible sons.

In retrospect, she must have seen me coming a mile away. I was the well-known lonely only son of one of New York City's most successful businessmen. And talk about low-hanging fruit. Ever since the mother I adored died when I was thirteen, I'd more or less walked through life with the words "single and desperate for the love of a good woman" tattooed on my forehead. So for someone like me to meet someone like Greta? A woman who spent her days teaching the neediest of children, and her nights bouncing from gala to gala nobly raising money for their educations? She was my dream come true. And for Greta to meet a desperate sucker like me? I was her dream come true.

I knew that I'd been had. And Dad knew that I knew it. But if I had inherited just one characteristic from my father, it was stubborn pride. I was willing to admit to myself that Greta was a gold digger, but that didn't mean I had to admit it to him.

Dad nudged me with his elbow. "Take another look at her," he said, nodding to the redhead whose boobs had triggered this whole awful conversation. "Tall. Stacked. Gorgeous from head to toe. That's the kind of woman you want at your side when *Forbes* is taking your picture. That's the kind of woman who will get you places in this world."

"You're saying I should find myself a trophy wife?"

"No," he said. "I'm saying there are two kinds of women in this world. Pretty bitches and ugly bitches. Both will be more interested in the divorce settlement than they will be in the marriage, so you may as well marry the one with the blondest hair and the biggest boobs. If possible, get one with blue eyes. And make sure she's at least fried fish upon a derby."

"Make sure she's *what?*"

Dad came in close and spoke loudly into my left ear. "At least five six and under thirty!" He pulled back and reverted to a normal voice. "What did you think I said?"

"I don't remember."

"Bullshit. Have you made an appointment with an audiologist yet? I'm getting sick of having to repeat everything I say."

"I'm only thirty years old," I said. "I don't need a hearing aid. Yet."

"Stop fighting it, son. It's nothing to be ashamed of. Your mother started wearing hers when she was fourteen and she was never embarrassed about it."

I swallowed the rest of my ginger ale and gestured to the bartender for the check before my father had a chance to say another word about my departed mother. As far as I was concerned, there were certain topics of conversation that were off-limits to him, and she was one of them.

"Leaving so soon?" Dad said.

I held up my phone. "It's ten o'clock. Our hour's up."

We stood and gave each other a sterile hug.

"Love you, son."

"Love you, Dad."

It was a beautiful May night. If I weren't so depressed, I'd have gone for a nice long walk. But all I wanted to do was get home, climb under the covers, and completely forget the conversation I'd just had with my damned father.

But I couldn't. And it wasn't just about Greta. It was about Megan. And Ilsa. And every other woman I'd stupidly believed cared about me, only to find out she only cared about my money. Correction. Cared about my father's money. I wasn't the billionaire. I was just the billionaire's son. Take Dad out of the picture, and I was just a lowly software developer who earned a few hundred thousand a year and had maybe ten mill in inherited assets.

But thanks to my media whore of a father, everyone who followed the Manhattan social scene knew about the incredible wealth I stood to inherit. As I walked down the block to my car, Dad's words about the kind of woman a man like me was doomed to attract played over and over again in my head. *They'll be more interested in the divorce settlement than they will be in the marriage.* I didn't agree that all women were bitches who only cared about money, but historically the women I attracted certainly fit the profile. By virtue of lineage, I was automatically prey for the most manipulative of predators, and the number of female con artists I'd been roped in by stood at three. How many other brilliant actresses were out there waiting to reel me in like a fish and make a complete fool of me? Maybe Dad was right. If all women wanted from me was money, maybe I *should* go for the trophy. Maybe I should just chase after big-bosomed, blue-eyed babes who knew how to smile for the photographers at *Forbes*.

As I was pondering the possibility of spending the rest of my life with someone endowed with two enormous jugs but not a single brain cell, I spotted my car. Pulling my keys out of my pocket, I clicked the unlock button on my keychain.

But I didn't hear the usual beep-beep. Sonofabitch. I'd left the doors unlocked on the New York City streets *again.* The whole reason I traded in my hundred-and-fifty-thousand-dollar Mercedes for an older, inconspicuous Toyota was so that I wouldn't attract gold diggers. But in place of the gold diggers, I was going to attract car thieves. I should just start leaving my keys in the ignition to make their jobs easier.

I walked over to the driver's side and pulled the handle. But no sooner had I opened the door than I noticed something unusual.

High heels. Ripped black fishnet stockings. A skintight miniskirt and equally skintight red blouse. And a head of blond hair face down on my steering wheel.

What I knew for sure was that a strange woman was in my car. What I didn't know was whether she was dead or alive. Placing one hand lightly under her chin and grasping her hair in the other, I gently pulled back her head to reveal a lipstick-smeared face.

"A moment of clarity," the woman said in an inebriated voice. "Get it? Clara-ty?"

I didn't get it. I let go of her hair, and her face fell back on the steering wheel with a resounding thud. "Excuse me?" I said, shaking her shoulder and hoping she wasn't dripping nosebleed blood all over my upholstery. "Miss?"

But there was no response. She was out cold. A drunken prostitute was unconscious in my car. One well-timed photo by a greedy paparazzo could put a half-million-dollar dent in my father's annual hush-money budget. Shit. Shit, shit, shit.

Oh, and one more thing.

Shit.

CHAPTER 3

Clara

A steering wheel was on my face. Or rather, my face was on a steering wheel.

I sat up, massaging the dents the wheel had left in my forehead, and peered outside. I was still on 63rd Street. The sun was just beginning to rise, which meant there was a very good chance my mother was still at the bar. Maybe I could text her and ask her to bring me a coffee. Make that an espresso. Two espressos. God, my head was killing me.

"Good morning, sunshine," a voice said.

I jumped, then whirled toward the passenger seat, where a very pissed-off-looking man of about thirty was sitting.

"I see we're up and ready to start our day," he said.

Brown hair. Brown eyes. Looked like he hadn't shaved in twenty-four hours, but very well dressed in neatly pressed khakis and a baby blue shirt with the top button unbuttoned. Not drop dead gorgeous, but not bad looking either.

"Do I know you?" I said.

"You'd certainly think so, what with you taking the liberty of sleeping one off in my car. But no, we're meeting for the first time." Smiling disingenuously, he waved goodbye. "Thank you for joining me in my car for the entire fucking night. I've truly enjoyed our time together, but I'm afraid it's time for you to leave and never return."

"This isn't my car?" I said, looking down at the seat beneath my hungover ass. The upholstery was fine black leather, whereas the upholstery in my car was fine green duct tape. I raised my eyes. There was a state-of-the-art sound and navigation system built into the dashboard, whereas my car's dashboard sported a state-of-the-art bullet hole (courtesy of the previous owner, something about a drug dealer with poor business etiquette). Nope, this was definitely not my car.

I turned my attention to the car's rightful owner. "It's a pleasure to meet you," I said for lack of something better to say. Speaking of pleasure, it occurred to me that there was a very awkward question I needed to ask. "I'm sorry, did we—"

"Fornicate?" he said. "No. I prefer my women sober. And conscious. And free-of-charge. I'm old-fashioned that way."

"Then how'd I end up here?"

"Don't know, don't care," he said. "All I know is that I had a drink at Geppetto's last night, and when I returned to my car at ten o'clock, you were sitting in my driver's seat very ironically saying the words 'a moment of clarity.'"

Vaguely, I remembered thinking that "clarity" sounded like my name. Clara-ty. It seemed really funny at the time. Not so much now.

I tried to make a joke of it. "Well, thank you for not calling the police on me or pushing me out of the car onto the sidewalk."

"Is that how most of your dates end?"

The stranger whose car I had broken into was starting to get on my nerves. "I wasn't on a date! I was having a drink. With my mother."

He pretended to look around the car. "Funny, I don't see her anywhere. Should I check the trunk?"

"You know what?" I said, increasingly annoyed by his rudeness. "I'm really sorry I did whatever I did that made me end up in your car instead of mine. I get that I inconvenienced you and that this is all my fault, but your sarcasm isn't helping."

"Inconvenienced," he repeated. "Interesting choice of words."

I grabbed my purse from the console. "I'll be out of your hair in a minute. Let me just find my . . ." I began digging through my purse. "Crap, do you see my car keys anywhere? They must have fallen out of my bag."

We both began looking around, under the seats, in the cup holders, and in the glove compartment. But our search came up empty. "Are you sure you had them on you?" the man said. "Maybe you—oh, for God's sake."

"What?"

He pointed toward the steering wheel.

Hanging from his ignition was a dodo bird-shaped keychain.

My keychain. I had evidently been so drunk that I had attempted to drive off in someone else's car. An embarrassed heat rising to my face, I grabbed my key chain and pulled. Then pulled again. And then one last time for good measure.

But it was no use. My keys and his ignition had become one, united together in love for all eternity.

"Please tell me this is a joke," he said.

I hid my face in my hands. God, this was humiliating. "I'm really, really sorry," I said, peeking through my fingers. But he wasn't looking at me. His elbows were on his knees, his head in his hands, and he was mumbling. I couldn't quite make out his words, but I assumed he was saying something to the effect of: *How have I offended thee, oh Lord, that thou hath smote me with this horrible woman?*

He flopped back against the seat, his eyes staring blankly out the windshield. I might have been imagining it, but his face had gone pale, almost gray, like he'd given up all hope in life. I usually didn't have that effect on a man until at least the fourth date.

"I'm really sorry," I repeated. "I know it's not much of a peace offering, but since we're stuck here, can I at least buy you a bagel? Or coffee? Or anything just to get us out of this car before it gets any worse?"

He turned to me, his eyes pleading. "Oh my God, it could get worse?"

"No, no, of course not," I said. "I just meant that—"

Before I could finish, something smacked against the windshield. The meter maid walked away without wishing us a nice day.

We both tilted our heads to read the damage on the orange-and-white parking ticket.

A hundred and forty dollars.

"I can pay for that," I said. It was a lie. I rescued birds from polluted wetlands for a living. I couldn't even afford the theoretical bagel I'd offered to buy him. But it seemed like the right thing to say.

"No!" he said, his annoyance returning full force. "For the love of God, please don't do me any favors."

"It's my fault you got a parking ticket, why shouldn't I—"

"Because I want to live, that's why. If I spend one more second with you, a meteor is going to land on my car and kill us both and one of us doesn't deserve to die today!" He pulled his wallet out of his back pocket and started thumbing through it. "Here," he said, trying to hand me four one hundred-dollar bills. "Just take it and leave, okay?"

When I didn't take it, he stuffed the cash into the side pocket of my purse, reached across me, and pulled the handle of the driver's side door. "It's been real," he said, pushing it open. "Let's do it again sometime. Ta."

No sooner had I stepped onto the sidewalk than he climbed into his driver's seat and slammed the door shut. I knocked on the window.

"Can I at least give you my address so you can mail me my keys?"

He rolled down his window. "Four hundred not enough?" he said, evidently not having heard a word I said. He reached into his pocket and pulled out some more cash. "Here," he said, handing me two wrinkled singles through the car window. "It's every last penny I have on me."

I came very close to stuffing the two singles, along with the four hundreds, down the sonofabitch's throat. But four hundred and two dollars was four hundred dollars more than I had in my bank account, and I wasn't in a fiscal position to be self-righteous or proud. I only wished every man who wanted to get rid of me gave me money with his parting words. I'd be a rich woman.

I stomped across the street to the only open store on the block, a very grungy twenty-four-hour bodega.

I was mad. At myself. At vodka. At the gods of about ten different religions. At the stranger who paid me four hundred and two bucks just to get me out of his car. But mostly at Tyler. I should be spending today joyfully dotting my i's and crossing my t's and making sure every little detail was perfect so that my wedding day was everything I ever dreamed it would be. Instead, I was in the toiletry aisle of a poorly lit convenience store at five thirty in the morning with nothing to my name but four hundred dollars and a twenty-year-old car that was, at the moment, missing in action. Perhaps it was in a back alley somewhere, serving as the new home for a band of thieves. Or perhaps the police, taking one look at it, had assumed it was a crime scene and towed it to their forensics lab for meth testing. If so, I didn't blame them.

But first things first—my mouth felt like I had eaten a rat pelt for breakfast, and my head felt like someone had struck it with a crowbar. I tossed a two-pack of Excedrin into my handbasket, along with a travel toothbrush kit, a bar of soap, and a packet of wipes. And last but not least, a can of cold espresso.

I brought my goods to the register. "Nine-fifty," said the cashier.

I handed him a hundred-dollar bill.

"Do you have anything smaller?"

"Sorry," I said.

"Then I'm going to have to give you change in small bills."

"That's fine," I said.

I waited patiently as he counted out ninety singles and five dimes. The sun was completely up by the time the transaction was complete.

"Is there a bathroom I can use?" I asked.

"Past the ice-cream freezer."

I headed to the back of the store. When I opened the bathroom door, I almost passed out from disgust. There was so much dried pee on the toilet seat that you could barely read the word *gonorrhea* written across it in green Sharpie. But despite the sights so bad you could smell them and smells so bad you could hear them, I was never so happy to gingerly squat over a toilet in my life. Or to brush my teeth. There were multiple reasons I avoided alcohol, and the diuretic effect and morning-after breath were in the top five. After brushing the fur off my tongue, I downed a painkiller with a swig of coffee, and then washed my face. The hot water felt good. Wonderful even. I briefly considered taking a bath in the sink, but the basin was so small I'd have to bathe one ass cheek at a time; it was worth neither the effort nor the syphilis. So instead, I gave myself a very pathetic sponge bath with the wipes.

After pulling my hair into a ponytail, I rewarded myself with another well-earned Excedrin. Emotionally I was still a train wreck, but physically, at least, I looked okay.

I stepped out of the bathroom.

To find the stranger from the car waiting.

"Oh my God, you've got to be kidding me," he said.

I made a grand *entrez-vous* gesture at the opened bathroom door. "It was like this when I got here," I said. "Enjoy your visit."

He reluctantly entered, and I gladly departed.

I stepped out into the street. Now came the hard part. Finding my car. I looked across the street.

And found my car.

It was parked directly behind the stranger's car. I could see how, in my drunken state, I had confused the two. They were both blue, both coupes, and roughly the same shape and size. But his car, a Toyota, was about a hundred times nicer than my 1999 Mercury Cougar. Too bad I didn't go all the way and steal the damn thing.

The first thing I did after I climbed into the driver's seat—*my* driver's seat—was reach into the backseat for my backpack. My rescue work with Eco-Justice required a lot of drudging through swamps and marshlands, so I always kept a few changes of clothes in my car. Looking around to make sure no one could see me, I slipped out of my miniskirt and wiggled and jiggled my way into my jeans. I then slipped off my red blouse and grabbed my favorite cotton T-shirt. But just as I pulled it over my boobs, I realized I'd grabbed the wrong shirt. My favorite shirt bore a minimalist picture of an egret. The one I'd just put on said "Stop This Fracking Asshole" on it. I had personally designed it for Eco-Justice to raise funds for a lawsuit we were filing against a fracking start-up. The sale had been a huge success, with over ten thousand shirts sold at twenty dollars a pop. There was even one person who bought a hundred of them in a single order (a hundred and ten, actually—they were buy ten get one free). But I rarely wore mine. It wasn't designed for busty women and no matter what size I attempted to wear, the word "asshole" always ended up stretched out across my enormous boobs and was the only part of the shirt anyone ever noticed.

I folded it back up, returned it to my duffle bag, and grabbed my egret shirt. Then I kicked off my heels and slipped into a pair of loafers.

Ah, I looked like me again. Time to start eating like me again. I reached into the backseat and grabbed one of the six bakery boxes that were stacked on the floor. I'd always been a sucker for those stupid Valentine candy hearts, so for the wedding, I'd had this idea that instead of one gigantic cake, we'd have individual heart-shaped cupcakes, each with a cutesy expression on them—*4ever Yours, UR a QT, B Mine*, and so on. But they were a custom order and the bakery refused to cancel them. So I picked them up yesterday and decided to prove Tyler right by quite literally eating my feelings. It would be a purge, kind of like that urban legend about the father who makes his son smoke every single cigarette in the carton until the son never wants to see another tobacco product again. In the spirit of self-disgust, I would eat every single gooey feeling I ever felt for Tyler until I was so sickened by the thought of him that I'd never want to feel anything for him again.

I started with a white frosted cupcake with *B Mine* on it. Next, I ate a pink one that said *U & Me*. After eating my third cupcake and then a fourth, it became clear that my plan to eat until I was disgusted was never going to work. These tacky little cupcakes were the yummiest things I'd ever eaten. I decided then and there to revise my purge: I would eat so many cupcakes that I'd never fit into a wedding dress again. Fuck Tyler. Who needs a man when you have eleven pounds of frosting?

I finished off one last cupcake and returned the box to the top of the stack. Then, I bent over and felt around the underside of my seat for the spare key I kept taped there in case of emergencies. The back of my hand brushed some spare change, a few stray pencils, and a sanitary napkin. Dammit. The key had to be here somewhere. Maybe I'd put it in the glove box.

But when I sat up and reached for its handle, I spotted the man from the Toyota standing outside his car, grabbing his door handle. And pulling. And pulling again. He stuck his hand in his pants pocket, presumably digging around for his keys. He then searched his other pocket. I saw him bend over, cup his hands around his eyes to block out the glare, and peer through his window.

When he returned to a fully upright position, he raised his hands and eyes to the sky and mouthed, *Fuck me*. Dramatically. *Fuuu-uuu-uuck me.*

I knew exactly what was going on, as I'd made the very same plea to the heavens many times before. He'd locked his keys in his car.

I rolled down my window. "Is there something I can do to help?" I called.

He turned at the sound of my voice, shocked. I almost felt sorry for him. Every time he thought he'd seen the last of me, I reappeared. Poor bastard.

CHAPTER 4

IAN

God help me. Every time I thought I saw the last of this woman, she reappeared.

Her head was jutting out the window of a car that looked like a prop from the set of *Law & Order*. There was a hole in the hood where the emblem should be, and I could only assume there was a headless body in the trunk. Yet at the same time, I kind of understood how, in her drunken state, she could have mistaken my car for hers. Except for the part where my car was only five years old and hers looked like it had rolled off the lot sometime during the Eisenhower administration, they were eerily similar. It was as if her car were my car's great-grandfather.

I wasn't looking forward to what I had to do next. But a millionaire's gotta do what a millionaire's gotta do, and right now this millionaire had to borrow ten bucks from a prostitute. Lucky thing we were related via vehicular lineage. Otherwise it might have been awkward.

I walked over to her car and lowered my head to the window. "Do you have ten dollars I can borrow?" I said.

Reaching into her purse, she pulled out a massive wad of singles. "A man like you doesn't have a credit card?" she said as she counted out ten singles.

"I locked my wallet in my car," I said. "With my keys." Sigh. "And my phone."

She gave me ten dollars, all in singles. "Come back when you're done washing up," she said. "I'll drive you home."

No, she wouldn't. I took the money and headed back to the store. After paying the guy at the register, I returned to the ever-so-charming bathroom. In addition to the word "gonorrhea" on the toilet seat, I found no less than twelve phone numbers of women who were available for a good time circa 1985. But the fun didn't end there. If the Met ever decided to sponsor an exhibition called "Artistic Representations of Penises in New York City Public Toilets," there were some brilliant works to be found on the walls. The etching next to the mirror was quite possibly an original Cezanne. At any rate, the cubist interpretation was certainly an intriguing one.

After giving myself a quick shave with a disposable plastic razor, I brushed my teeth and washed my face. Wetting my hair, I combed it into shape with my fingers.

I stepped back out into the street. The early morning sun was now shining brightly, and I could see my friend the streetwalker waiting for me, her window open, her eyes looking down at her phone. I supposed it was thoughtful of her to wait for me, but no way in hell was I accepting her offer of a ride home in that duct-taped death trap on wheels. I had a few casual friends in the city. Surely one of them would be willing to drive me back to Connecticut. At home I had cash, credit cards, a land line, and anything else I needed to get myself out of this mess.

She waved to me out her window. "Ready to go?"

"Thanks, but I'm good!" I yelled as I headed toward my car. "I'm going to call a friend to pick me up."

She stuck her head out the window. "I thought you said you locked your phone in your car!"

I stopped in the middle of the street, my hands clenching into fists. Shit, shit, shit. As a rule, I was extremely gifted at taking things in stride; the only time I felt real anger was when I was with my father. But at the moment, I was freaking furious. And, for once in my life, not just at Dad. At Greta. At the nameless woman who'd passed out in my car. But mostly, at myself. If I hadn't carelessly neglected to lock my car last night, I wouldn't be in this ridiculous situation in the first place. Now I had to rely on a hooker to get myself out of it.

Unclenching my fists and taking a deep breath, I climbed inside the passenger seat of her car.

"So I guess I'll take that ride," I said, feigning a smile.

"Glad I can help," she said, giving me a smile back.

I couldn't help but notice that she looked different. Sometime between the convenience store and now, she had changed into jeans and a cotton T-shirt. Her long blond hair was in a simple ponytail, her face was clean of lipstick and mascara, and her eyes were no longer bloodshot. She was really quite attractive. Her skin was pale, her lashes long and lush, and her wide eyes a stunning blue.

She extended her hand. "Clara," she said. "Zapata."

Reluctantly, I shook. "Ian," I said. "Dun . . . Dunfordsomer."

I dodged the bullet just in time. I'd almost given her my real name. If she looked up Ian Dunning on the internet, she would find out that she had a prime candidate for blackmail sitting at her side. Many a hooker had made a killing off extorting a rich man. I wasn't about to become a victim.

"Well," she said as she let go, "it's a pleasure to meet you, Ian Dundunfordsomer. What kind of name is that? I've never heard it before."

The kind of name an idiot like me comes up with off the top of his head when he's trying to hide his true identity. In retrospect, I could have gone with Dunleavy. Or Dunham. Or just plain Dunne. Instead, I'd come up with Dunfordsomer. Oops, correction, Dundunfordsomer. This was why I could never follow in my father's footsteps and become a brilliant businessman. You had to be an adroit and remorseless liar, and I sucked at it. "Norwegian," I said.

"I would have guessed something Anglo-Saxon. How do you spell that?"

Beats the hell out of me. "Like it sounds. Hey, can we just get out of here? I've been here since ten last night and I'd like to get home by ten this morning."

My tone must have been harsher than I realized, because she seemed insulted. She handed me her phone. "If my company is not to your liking," she said, her voice stern, "call one of your friends and have them come pick you up."

"I don't know their numbers," I said. "When I want to call someone, I just hit their name." The only number I knew by heart was my father's, and no way in hell was I going to let him know how badly I'd fucked up.

"Call an Uber," she suggested.

"My credit card is in my car."

"I recently came into four hundred dollars. More than happy to share some of it."

"It won't be enough," I said.

"Four hundred dollars isn't enough to get you home? Where the hell do you live?

"Connecticut."

"I have to drive all the way to Connecticut with you?"

"I'm happy to pay you for your time," I said. "I have cash at home. Will three hundred dollars do the trick?"

She didn't look happy about this new development. But considering how she earned her money most days, I figured she had to be relieved to make a few bucks sitting upright in a car instead of lying supine on a bed.

"Is that on top of the four hundred and two you already gave me?" she asked.

"Yes."

"Fine," she said. "I'll drive you to Connecticut. Which way?"

"Take the FDR to I-95," I said. "I'll give you directions from there."

CHAPTER 5

CLARA

The way this jackass was acting, you'd think he was accepting a ride home from a hooker. Sure, my car was a third-world country on wheels, but at least it had unlocked doors and a functional ignition, so I didn't see what the big problem was. At any rate, he'd already made me feel plenty stupid and worthless, and sitting here acting like he was being forced to drive home in a public toilet wasn't making me feel any better.

"Can you please grab my spare key?" I said without looking at him. "I think it's in the glove compartment."

He reached for the glove box. And then suddenly stopped. "Holy crap, is that a—" He inserted his finger into the hole in my dashboard. "Is that a bullet hole?"

"No!" I said. "Of course not! It's a . . ." I shuffled through my bag until I found the ninety-nine-cent lipstick I'd bought from the dollar store. "It's a lipstick holder," I said. "All the old cars were made with them. See?" I stuck my lipstick in the bullet hole. A moment later we heard a clunk as it hit the hollow inner pit of my dashboard. "Lipstick cases were fatter when this car was manufactured," I explained.

"Whatever," he said.

"Fine, I'm lying, it's not a lipstick holder. It's—"

"Please don't explain," he said as he opened the glove box. "The less I know, the better."

He handed me the key and I turned it in the ignition. With the regular clunks, bangs, booms, and grunts, my car started up, and I pulled out of the parking space and headed out.

Even on a Saturday morning, New York City traffic was hell. By eight o'clock, we were only just crossing the border from Manhattan into the Bronx. I really had to pee.

I miraculously spotted an empty parking space and pulled in.

"Why are we stopping?" Ian said, as if I needed his written permission to take a rest stop.

"There's a grocery store at the end of the block," I said, pointing. "I need to use the bathroom."

He looked out the window at the splendor that was the South Bronx. "Here?" he said, horrified.

Clearly this was a man who'd never laid eyes on a housing project before. "No," I said. "In the grocery store. I'm thinking the produce aisle."

"Can't it wait until we get to a better neighborhood?"

"Don't worry," I said. "No one in their right mind would steal a car with an asshole like you inside it." I grabbed my bag. "Would you like me to get you a ham sandwich or is it beneath your dignity to have anything but caviar and Bichon Frise for breakfast?"

He looked at me like I was the dumbest person on earth. "I'm not hungry," he said. "And Bichon Frise is a dog breed."

"I knew that," I said, then made sure to slam the door behind me.

Dammit. I could have sworn Bichon Frise was a French cheese.

"Bathroom?" I said to a guy stacking apples by the entrance.

"Back left," he said without looking at me.

After a quick pee, I headed to the prepared food aisle. I'd eaten the equivalent of five slices of cake for breakfast so I wasn't exactly hungry, but I figured I should buy something for the road in case we hit more monster traffic. But when I got to aisle eight, I was disappointed to find Ian already there.

"I thought you said you weren't hungry."

His eyes were scanning the selection. "I suddenly had a craving for a Malamute sandwich. Maybe with a St. Bernard salad on the side."

I tried to think of something snotty to say in response. But the best I could come up with was: "Just find something. I'll go grab a couple of drinks. Is cola okay?"

"Ginger ale," he said with neither a please nor a thank you.

We met at the register, paid for our stuff, and stepped back outside. We were about fifty feet from my car when I noticed something.

"My windshield," I said.

"What about it?"

"It's gone."

"It's gone?" he said, incredulous.

I jogged down the block to my car, Ian following behind.

"Your windshield's gone," he said when he caught up.

"I know," I said.

"I don't understand. Shouldn't there be broken glass all over the place?"

"It's not broken," I said. "It's gone."

"It's gone?"

"It's gone," I repeated.

"Where did it go?"

"Nowhere on its own," I explained. "Someone stole it."

"Someone stole it?"

"Are you going to repeat everything I say?"

"I'm just trying to wrap my mind around the concept of windshield theft," he said. "That's a thing? Really?"

"They don't make cars like mine anymore so if something breaks, you can't buy the spare parts from the dealer," I explained. "Thieves look for cars that are no longer being manufactured, steal the obsolete parts, then sell them for a killing."

"In broad daylight?"

"Evidently."

"So what do we do?"

"We find the nearest used auto parts shop," I said. "We can't drive all the way to Connecticut without a windshield." I pulled up my phone browser and typed in *used auto parts near me*. The closest one was only about four blocks away. "I found one. Let's go."

As it turned out, even four blocks was a long way when it involved driving with the exhaust of a Pontiac Grand Am blowing directly into our faces.

"I can't breathe," Ian said, gagging.

"Just close your eyes and hold your breath for one more minute. We're almost there." I found a parking spot in front of the shop and pulled in. "Are you coming in or do you want to wait in the car?"

"Wait out here?" he said, aghast. "Alone? With no weapon?"

What a wimp. "Then let's go."

A feral-looking man with black grease streaks covering every exposed part of his body came to the front of the store as soon as we entered.

"Hello, there," he said. "What brings you folks in today?"

I really, really wasn't in the mood for this transaction. "I'm looking for a windshield for a 1999 Mercury Cougar," I said. "Do you happen to have one available?"

He placed his hands on his hips in a *well, I'll be darned* way. "You are not going to believe this," he said. "But wouldn't you know it, one got delivered here not more than fifteen minutes ago. This must be your lucky day."

"Must be," I said, already bored with the charade. "How much?"

"How much you got?"

No way was I playing this game. "How much?" I repeated.

"Two hundred."

"Not a chance," I said.

"One-fifty."

"I'll give you fifty," I said.

He crossed his arms over his chest, ready to play hardball. "One hundred," he said. "And I'll throw in the inspection sticker for free."

"That's very generous of you," I said. "Tell you what, throw in the inspection sticker *and* installation, and I'll give you one-twenty. Final offer."

He gave me a stare. But when he saw that I wasn't backing down, he broke into a smile. "You drive a hard bargain," he said. "Congratulations, you got a deal."

We followed him to the register.

"Could I interest you folks in a stereo today?" he said as he rang me up. "Ten percent off for first-time customers."

"No," I said. "Thank you."

"And will you be needing any license plates with your order?"

Son of a bitch. This guy had me exactly where he wanted me. I had two options: one, call the police and wait around three days for them to show up and do absolutely nothing, or two, play along. I decided to play along, if only to get Ian out of my life sooner. "I don't know," I said to the mechanic. "You tell me."

"I always say, you can't have enough license plates. If you like Georgia, I just got a shipment in yesterday. They got peaches on them."

"I think I'll stick to New York," I said.

"Any special number you had in mind?"

"I'm partial to JMR-436," I said. "You got anything in that model?"

He turned around and started thumbing through a crate behind the register.

"Well, would you look at that," he said, pulling two plates from the box. "This really is your lucky day. I just happen to have two New York plates with that exact number. Thirty bucks and they're all yours."

"Ten."

"Are you crazy?" he said. "This is a matching set in pristine condition. You know how hard it is to find—"

"Just give me my goddamned plates!" I said, slamming a hundred-dollar bill and thirty singles on the counter before grabbing the plates from his hand and storming back out to my car.

Like any other human being with a naturally occurring ego, I did not enjoy being made a fool of. But this was worse than your average humiliation. In addition to paying one hundred and thirty dollars to buy back my own car parts from the fucker who stole them in the first place, I was handing Ian an I-told-you-so opportunity on a silver platter. He'd told me not to park in this neighborhood, and I'd glibly ignored him. Now I was paying the price. Literally.

"Can you get me the screwdriver from the trunk?" I said.

He went to the back of my car and untaped the trunk. "Phillips or flathead?" he called.

"Flathead," I called back.

When he came around to the front, I reattached my license plates while my automotive professional reinstalled my windshield.

"All done!" Mr. Greasestreaks said a few minutes later. "Can we expect you back in the neighborhood anytime soon? Where do you usually park?"

"Fuck off!"

We had driven about two blocks when Ian evidently couldn't resist anymore. "I told you not to stop in that neighborhood."

"You couldn't wait to say that, could you?" I said as I turned right. "Good for you, you got your 'I told you so' in. Are you happy?"

"For what it's worth," he said. "I'm impressed."

"Impressed with what? Me being suckered into paying a hundred and thirty dollars to buy back my own stolen car parts?"

"It could have gone down a lot worse," he said. "I'm kind of thinking we got off easy, all things considered."

I kept my eyes on the road ahead. "I guess."

"So how much do we have left?"

"Gas?" I asked.

"Money."

"We spent about ten each at the convenience store," I said. "Then another ten at the grocery store. A hundred and thirty just now. And I'm going to have to pull off at that exit up there and fill the tank, so figure another forty or so. So two hundred left."

"Wow," he said. "All that math in your head. Impressive."

Was he serious? "It's basic addition and subtraction. A second grader could do it."

"I was just trying to pay you a compliment."

"Thanks," I said. "But congratulating me for being able to subtract two hundred from four hundred is actually really insulting."

"I just meant that most women like you aren't necessarily that good at math."

I was tempted to slam on the brakes and kick his ass out of my car. *Women like you.* I should be used to those words by now. After all, I'd been hearing them all my life. You're pretty. You have big boobs. Pretty plus titty equals dummy. It was a self-evident truth to sexist, shallow pricks everywhere: if she's attractive, she's stupid.

"I can also read," I said. "Even big words with a whole bunch of letters. Look, there are some now," I said, pointing to the Connecticut sign. "Con . . . conukticat? Did I read that right? No, wait. Connec . . . Connecty-cut. Ooooh, that sounds like a fun country. Let's go there. I've never been to Europe before."

"Sorry," he said. "I won't make the mistake of trying to be nice to you again."

"Using the word 'nice' a little loosely these days, aren't we?"

"I won't say another word for the rest of the trip, will that make you happy?"

"That would make me ecstatic," I said. "Thank you."

I stepped harder on the gas pedal, breaking seventy-five miles an hour. The sooner I got this bastard home and out of my life forever, the better.

CHAPTER 6

IAN

We spent the next two hours in silence. When I needed her to take an exit or make a turn, I pointed. But now that we were only a few miles from my house, we were at the point where I needed to give verbal directions.

"Am I allowed to open my mouth?" I said. "Just to give you directions?"

She slowed down to thirty miles an hour as we turned right into a residential neighborhood. "Fine."

"Next left."

She followed my directions, turning left and right and left and right down the long series of twisting roads that led to my driveway.

"This is me," I said.

"Your street?" she said, looking around for a sign.

"My driveway."

She looked a little surprised. And why wouldn't she be? Most people's driveways weren't a mile long. I wondered if she was starting to see dollar signs yet. If so, she was going to be disappointed when we got to the end of my driveway and she saw my simple, thousand-square-foot house.

We continued in silence until we reached my waterfront cottage. She had a perplexed expression on her face as she pulled into the parking space. "Can I make an observation?" she asked.

Our journey was mercifully nearing its end, so I didn't see any harm in allowing her a few last utterances before we said goodbye forever. "Sure."

"The dimensions of your driveway are deceptively disproportionate to the size of your house. I was expecting a mansion."

She turned to me for a response, but I said nothing. I was a little taken aback by the literacy of the sentence. *The dimensions are deceptively disproportionate . . .* In addition to being the best-looking and most mathematically proficient hooker in history, she had an excellent vocabulary. But when I complimented her on her math earlier, she'd nearly bitten my head off. She'd probably kill me on the spot if I congratulated her on her wordsmithing.

I decided to keep my response simple. "The previous owner liked his privacy."

She looked toward the water. "Looks like he certainly got what he wanted."

Without another word, she stepped out of the car, and I followed suit.

"So," she said over the hood of her car, "can I get my three hundred bucks now?"

Ah, back to hooker-speak.

"Yeah," I said, "let me run inside, I'll be back in a sec."

When we reached the porch, she paused. "I like the way the façade faces the water," she said. "Nice sunrises, I suppose."

"I guess," I said as I typed the security code into the keypad.

Beeeeep went the "wrong code" alarm. I typed in the six-digit code again. And once again got the alarm. "Shit," I mumbled.

"What's wrong?" Clara said.

"I changed the security code last week," I said. "I'm sure I'm typing it in right but it's not letting me in."

"Didn't you write it down anywhere?"

"It's in my phone."

"Which is—"

"Still sitting in my car on 63rd Street." I typed the code in one more time, only to hear one more beep. "Goddammit."

"Is there any other way to get in?" she said.

There was not. Daddy Dearest insisted on paying a security company three thousand dollars a month—that's right, a *month*—to make my house an impenetrable fortress. Clara didn't know it, but my mile-long driveway was lined with hidden security cameras. There were even cameras on the beach side of my property to spot potential kidnappers inclined to approach by boat. And every single door, window, and even the chimney practically had its own armed guard. Without the code, there was no way we were getting in.

"We're screwed," I said.

"Do you have the number of the security company?"

"I can only verify my identity through an app."

"Which is, let me guess—"

"On my phone."

There was probably a workaround, but the fact was, I didn't even know the name of the security company.

My father's minions took care of all that for me. It was one of those moments when I really, really wished I wasn't my father's son. But then again, every moment was a moment when I wished I wasn't my father's son. But some moments of my miserable life were more miserable than others, and this was quickly shaping up to be one of them.

"I need to pee," Clara said.

"What else is new?"

"It's at critical mass."

I made a sweeping gesture to the wooded lands around my property. "The world is thy toilet. Plenty of rocks to hide behind."

"Fine," she said with a huff.

After retrieving a roll of toilet paper from her trunk (I made a point of not asking the backstory there), she scampered off to the woods to pee in blissful ignorance of the CCTV cameras in the trees overhead. For my part, I headed to the shed to fetch my spare car key.

I hadn't been inside it since last fall and it was so dusty and musty and spider-webby that it almost seemed haunted. But as I made my way through, I encountered no ghosts, just the regular guy-stuff collection of tools and boxes and things with wheels.

Pulling the collar of my shirt over my nose, I headed toward the corner where I kept my spare key hidden. But after only one step forward, my foot accidently kicked something that caused a domino effect. It started with a snow shovel falling off its wall hook, then something landing on my head, followed by me tripping and grabbing a wall shelf for support. The grand finale was the wall shelf and everything on it crashing to the floor.

Through it all, I miraculously suffered minimal damage to the general cranial region.

The back end of the shed did not fare as well, however. Its injuries were grievous. It looked like it alone had been struck by an earthquake. Sometime this weekend, I'd have a jolly good time cleaning up the wreckage, but for now all I needed to do was unearth my key. I kicked a few small crates and hand tools out of my way as I forged a path through the rubble. I was just pushing aside the contents of a broken cardboard box when something caught my eye.

A ghost.

My heart skipped a beat. But not because I was scared. The ghost in question was anything but an unwelcome one. And it wasn't your run-of-the-mill, garden-variety ghost, the kind that passes through walls and floats above your head singing "la la la, la la la" in a creepy little girl's voice just to fuck with you.

No, this ghost was of the most mundane variety: a child's notebook. It was standard fare, black with white speckles. Under the words "Composition Book" were three lines of adolescent handwriting.

Ian Dunning, Grade 8
Mom's Memory Book
Private Property Do Not Read

I could barely believe it. My long-lost memory book. I'd misplaced it over a decade ago and it had been years since I'd even allowed myself to hope I'd ever find it again.

I picked it up. The last time I'd seen it was the day before I left for college. I'd planned to bring it to Tufts with me, but paranoid visions of drunken dorm mates finding it and reading it aloud as part of a fraternity prank made me think the better of it. But then again, if I left it at home, there was the danger that one of my father's underpaid household servants would find it and make a beeline to the nearest cash-paying tabloid. The gossip-mongering press would pay extremely good money to get their hands on Dunning family drama in any form, and what could be more dramatic than a poor little rich boy's journal of memories of his dead mother? The sad truth was, my journal, and the secrets and emotions and love hidden in its pages, was worth its weight in gold. It wasn't safe anywhere, and no one on earth could be trusted with it. So I'd hidden it away in a super-secret hiding place where there was no chance anyone would ever find it.

Including me. I'm what people like my father like to call "book smart, life stupid." I can do complex math in my head and I'm fluent in multiple computer languages, but if someone says, *How're you doing*, I'm known to respond with *Thanks!* When I'm running out the door, there's a good chance I'll miss the door. And the only time I remember to lock my car is when my keys, phone, and wallet are inside it. In short, it was extremely like me to hide my notebook so brilliantly that even I couldn't find it.

I spent the entirety of my first Christmas home from college scouring all eight thousand square feet of the house for the notebook. I searched each and every room, including the bathrooms, top to bottom. But it was no use. My journal, and all the memories buried inside it, was gone. It was the first time since my mother died that I actually cried.

But now here it was. How it had ended up in a cardboard box in my unlocked shed, I didn't know or care. All that mattered was that, after twelve long years, it was returned from the dead and back in my arms.

Yeah, I said in my arms. I was quite literally hugging it. One hundred percent of the only unconditional love I'd ever gotten from another human being was locked away in these pages. If ever there was such a thing as a living, breathing college-ruled notebook, this was it.

A little nervously, I opened to the very first page.

> *Mom died three weeks ago. My school counselor gave me this notebook and said I should write down all my memories of Mom before I forget them. I told him I didn't want to, but he says I don't ever have to show it to anyone else and I'll be glad I wrote everything down when I'm older.*

It was amazing how quickly the memories came flooding back. I was suddenly transported to my lonely private room at my new boarding school in Massachusetts. I could still remember writing the very first word of the very first entry. I was scared one of the other kids would find the journal and tell the other eighth graders I still used the word "Mommy," so I erased the last "m" and "y" and left it as "Mom." And then I felt guilty about feeling embarrassed, and then I wished my mom was there to tell me not to be embarrassed for missing her or scared of what other people might think.

That first year of boarding school was hell. I was lonely and sad, and ashamed of being lonely and sad. So I wrote. And wrote and wrote and wrote. By the last day of eighth grade, I had aged about five years. I could still remember the very last words I'd written. They were the last words Mom had ever spoken to me, and they were a promise. Maybe if I saw the words scribbled out in my childish handwriting, I'd feel the way I used to feel when I read Mom's promise to me. Safe. Hopeful. Loved.

But I couldn't bring myself to flip to the last page. Not here, not now. Not when Clara would be returning from her woodland pee any minute.

I heard the sound of leaves crunching under feet outside. Tiptoeing across the shed, I found an oversized Tupperware full of loose nails and screws. As quietly as possible, I emptied the contents into an empty burlap sack. Then I put the notebook inside the Tupperware and sealed the lid. As soon as this ordeal was over, I intended to lock myself in my room like a teenager and read my memory book cover to cover.

After putting the Tupperware on a low shelf, I found the bucket and grabbed my spare car key. Then I headed back outside.

Clara was standing at the spot where the surf met the sand, looking out over the quiet waters of the Long Island Sound.

"Do you get a lot of sandpipers?" she asked me when I reached her side.

"You mean those weird little birds that run away from the water?"

"Those are the ones." She turned to me, as if expecting me to offer some additional details on the local bird population. But the minute she saw me, her brows dipped in concern. "Holy crap, what the hell happened to you?"

"Oh," I said, figuring the falling shelf had drawn some blood. "I tripped in the shed. I must have gotten a scratch. Am I bleeding?"

"No," she said. "But your hands are shaking. You're pale as death. You look like you just saw a ghost."

Shit. I was breaking one of the Dunning family cardinal rules: *Don't let them see you sweat.* When you had the kind of money my family had, displays of emotion sent predators into a feeding frenzy. Loneliness was to gold diggers what blood was to sharks. Vulnerability. Weakness. An opportunity to pounce and eat you alive. The fact was, I *had* just seen a ghost. But I couldn't let Clara know that.

"A little anemia," I quickly improvised. "I didn't take my iron supplement this morning. I'll be fine."

I could tell she wasn't convinced, but she didn't argue, presumably because she didn't actually care one way or other. "If you say so," she said, shrugging. "Any luck with the security code?"

"No," I said. "But I did find my spare car key. So at least I can get back into my car."

"Well, I guess that's good news," she said. But then a puzzled look crossed her face. Followed by a terrified look.

"What?" I said.

"How exactly are you planning to get back to the city?"

Did I mention I'm book smart, life stupid? You'd think it would have occurred to me that some mode of transportation would be necessary to get back to my car. But it hadn't. Not once.

I faked a smile. "Sooo," I said, playing nice, "how'd you like to earn another three hundred dollars?"

This poor woman. Every time she thought she'd finally gotten rid of me, I came back from the dead.

"I mean, you have to drive back to the city anyway, right?" I said.

She started scurrying toward her car.

I chased behind her. "I can't give you the money I already owe you without my wallet!" I called. "Three hundred easy dollars just to let me sit in your passenger seat for a few more hours!"

"No!" she yelled, breaking into a sprint.

"Five hundred!" I called.

"I'd rather eat fried frog's ass!"

"Six hundred! You can't just leave me here, Clara! You have the only roll of toilet paper!"

She jumped into the driver's seat and began backing out. But I was quick, too, and jumped into the passenger seat while the car was moving. I couldn't let her leave without me.

Her tense hands gripped the steering wheel. "Fine," she said through clenched teeth. "I'll drive you. But I'm going to need a promissory note."

"You want to consult a lawyer before you'll drive me back to the city?"

"I didn't realize a promissory note was something that required a lawyer. I just meant that I need it in writing that you're going to pay me."

"I can do that," I said, willing to agree to anything if it meant she would drive me back to Manhattan. "Do you have a pen and a piece of paper?"

She dug around in her bag and pulled out a pen. "Just a minute," she said. She bent down, feeling around under her car seat. "Okay," she said, sitting up. "Use this."

She handed me the pen. And a sanitary napkin.

"Use it for what?" I said.

"I can't find a piece of paper."

For the first and last time in my life, I unwrapped a sanitary napkin from its pink wrapper. And for the first and last time in anyone's life, I wrote a legally binding contract on one.

I, Ian Dundunfordsomer, being of sound mind and body, hereby promise to pay Clara Zapata a sum total of one thousand dollars for services rendered upon this fourth day of May, the year of our Lord two-thou—"

"Very funny," she said, grabbing the napkin out of my hand before I had a chance to finish.

"Did you need to have that notarized?" I asked.

"You have your fingerprints and handwriting all over a Kotex," she said as she folded up the world's most sanitary promissory note and inserted it into her purse. "I'm pretty sure paying me will be easier than living down the notoriety you'll achieve if I post this on Insta to get even with you for reneging on your pledge."

"Is that a threat?"

"It most certainly is."

Without another word, she turned the key in the ignition, put the car into drive, and headed up my long driveway and back toward the city.

CHAPTER 7

Clara

Watching this asshole write out a financial promise on a super absorbent maxi pad with wings was the most fun I'd had all day. When this was all over, I planned to pull the sticky strip off the napkin and hang it on my wall like a painting. While it would unfortunately be the finest piece of artwork in my crappy apartment, on the plus side, it would make an excellent conversation piece for years to come.

At the same time, I felt a little bit guilty. There was such a thing as taking a joke too far, and Ian hadn't spoken a word since we'd left his house. After almost an hour of complete silence, I felt compelled to make peace. Or at least break the ice just a little.

"You can use my phone if you want to listen to some music," I said.

"Thanks," he said. "Maybe I will."

"Passcode is 544445."

He took my phone from the console and scrolled through my playlist. It was probably a full five minutes before he spoke again. "You have really good taste in music."

If I wasn't mistaken, Ian was suggesting we had something in common. It felt weird.

"What kind of music do you usually listen to?" I asked. Part of me hoped he'd say something like *Justin Bieber, the early years* to cancel out the awkward positivity floating around the car. I wanted to make peace with him, not friends with him. The mere suggestion that we had something in common was freaking me out.

"I'm a big Ben Harper fan," he answered.

Shit. "Me too," I reluctantly admitted.

"Obviously. You have all his albums on here. Which is your favorite?"

"*Welcome to the Cruel World.*"

"Hmm," he said. "Mine too."

Damn. Two things in common. I was afraid to ask my next question. "Favorite song?" I said, wincing. *Please don't let it be 'Forever,' please don't let it be 'Forever.'*

"'Forever.'"

No! Not one thing, not two things, but three things in common. Favorite singer, favorite album, favorite song. I felt like I had fleas. Maybe I'd luck out with film or books. "What about movies? Any favorite genre?"

He shrugged. "Typical guy stuff, I guess," he said. "Action. Thrillers."

Thank God. I hated both action and thrillers. The we-have-so-much-in-common cooties started jumping off me.

"What about you?" he asked.

"Typical girl stuff," I said. "Romantic comedy. Period pieces. But Leonardo DiCaprio's my favorite actor and I pretty much love anything he's in. Even an action movie. Doesn't really matter the genre."

"Did you see *Once Upon a Time in Hollywood?"* he asked, the conversation beginning to become uncomfortably friendly again. "I watched it a few weeks ago. It was really good."

"I saw it in the theater when it first came out," I said. "But only because Leo was in it. I wasn't crazy about the movie itself, but I enjoyed watching it because of him."

Ian looked at me, bewildered. "You *what?"*

"I wasn't crazy about the storyline. But I love Leo and I enjoyed watching it because of him."

He just stared at me like he couldn't believe anyone would ever even *think* such a thing, much less say it out loud. "Can you please say that again?"

Wow, talk about overreacting. "I said I enjoyed watching it because of him. Why do you keep making me repeat myself?"

"Because you can't possibly be saying what I think you're saying."

"Why not?"

"Because it makes absolutely no sense."

"It makes no sense that I didn't like the storyline of *Once Upon a Time in Hollywood* but I enjoyed watching it because of him?"

A light finally seemed to go off in his head. "You enjoyed watching it because of him?" he said. "That's what you said? That's what you've been saying this whole time?"

"Yes," I said. "God, why is that so hard for you to believe?"

"Because this whole time I thought you were saying *I was George Washington because of him."*

"You thought *what?"*

"I thought you said *I didn't like the movie but I was George Washington because of him.* I've never been so confused in my whole life."

I slowed the car to twenty and pulled onto the shoulder.

"Why are we stopping?" he said.

Putting the car into park, I dropped my head onto the steering wheel. My whole body began to convulse. I tried to speak but couldn't get the words out.

"Are you laughing at me so hard you can't drive?" Ian said.

Finally, I managed to lift my head off the steering wheel and spit out one word. "Yes."

When I say "spit," I mean there was actually airborne saliva involved. As my body continued to shake, I felt a single tear run down my face. Then another. Then another.

"You're laughing at me so hard you're crying?"

I nodded. "Yes," I barely managed to say. "Yes, I am."

As I continued my convulsive laughter, I could see Ian fighting a smile. "Fine," he conceded, starting to laugh himself. "I guess it's kind of funny." After a few seconds, he began to laugh in earnest. "Okay, it's really funny."

After about another minute or so, we were finally both calm enough that I felt comfortable driving again.

"I have to tell you," I said as I pulled back onto the highway, "I'm really not digging this thing where we're smiling and laughing and enjoying each other's company. Can you do something that will make me hate you again?"

His expression suddenly turned serious. Just barely, I heard a sigh.

"I could introduce you to my father."

CHAPTER 8

IAN

"Wow," she said. "That bad?"

As soon as the words left my mouth, I regretted them. I didn't want Clara to know who my father was, and not just because of the blackmail opportunity. In thirty years, the only person who ever really saw and loved me for me was my mother. Everyone else judged me through the filter of my father. They took the old adage "Like father, like son" as gospel truth. Dad's fame, wealth, and ego were a stain I could never wash off. I'd never be just plain old Ian Dunning. I'd always be Ian Dunning, only son and heir of tycoon Daniel Dunning.

But Clara had no idea who I really was. To her, I was just an ordinary guy. I didn't care if she hated me. Correction—I didn't care *that* she hated me. In lieu of being loved for who I was, I was happy to be hated for who I was. And in order to be loved or hated for the real me, I had to keep my lineage a secret.

"No," I said. "We just had a disagreement last night and I guess I'm still a little pissed. Forget I said it."

"No way," she said. "You can't just cut me off there."

"Slow down," I said. "You're driving too fast. And keep both hands on the wheel."

"Both my hands are on the wheel and I'm going ten miles below the speed limit."

"I know," I said. "But you asked me to do something to make you hate me again, so I'm being an obnoxious backseat driver."

"So you're just making stuff up about my driving so you don't have to tell me about your father?"

"There's nothing to tell," I said. I then told the biggest lie of my adult life. "We disagree on a few things, but we mostly get on great. He's a really good dad. You'd like him."

"Fine, then," she said. "I guess I don't get to hate you anymore. But can I still dislike and distrust you?"

"It would be my honor to be disliked and distrusted by you," I said. "But now it's your turn."

"My turn for what?"

"I'm starting to find you tolerable as well," I said. "I did something to make you re-hate me, now you have to do something to make me re-hate you."

"But yours didn't work," she said. "It kind of made me like you more."

"Effort, Clara. It's all about the effort. Try to make me hate you. Show me I'm worth it."

"Fine," she said. "Give me a minute."

As she continued to drive at fifty-five miles an hour, both hands on the wheel, she pondered which of her hateable qualities to share with me.

"Okay," she finally said. "I think I've got one."

"Lay it on me."

"I drive a 1999 Mercury Cougar with a bullet hole in the dashboard."

"I already hated you for that. You have to give me new material to work with."

"Okay, Mr. Fussy," she said. "Let me think."

"I'll be here when you're ready."

"I'm ready."

"Wow, that was fast."

"But you have to promise not to jump out of the car while it's moving."

"You have my word," I said.

"You asked for it," she said. "So here it is. I'm from New Jersey."

I jokingly grasped my heart. "Oh, God," I said. "It hurts. Can I take back what I said about not jumping out of the car?"

"Absolutely not," she said. "I already have to dish out a hundred and forty bucks for a parking ticket. Imagine what it will cost to scrape your carcass off the road and have it towed back to Manhattan. In case you haven't noticed yet, I'm kind of cash-strapped."

I'd noticed. It was kind of hard to miss.

Which raised an interesting question. How much did she charge for her services? I'd noticed earlier how attractive she was. But now that she was smiling and laughing, she was more than attractive. She was pretty. As in really, really pretty. I could proudly say that I never paid a woman for sex, so I didn't actually know the going rate for a high-end escort, but surely a woman like Clara—pretty, well-endowed in the chest area, and seemingly drug-free—could easily make thousands of dollars a night. Seriously. Hundreds of thousands of dollars a year. So why would she choose to be a common streetwalker?

"Can I ask you something personal?" I said.

She looked a little worried. "Yes?"

"And tell me if it's none of my business. But I'm just curious—what exactly made you choose your particular career path?"

She shrugged. "I didn't. It chose me."

"How do you mean?"

"I don't think I had a choice in the matter. It had always just been a hobby," she said. "Or not a hobby. More of a . . . I can't think of the word."

"A passion?"

"Yeah," she said. "A passion. But until I was eighteen, I never did anything about it. It was always just something I watched from the windows."

"You watched from the windows?" I said. Maybe her neighbors in Jersey were perverts who left their curtains open on purpose.

"Or when I was walking through the woods," she continued. "Or even just in the park, looking up into the trees and admiring from afar. It was all just so beautiful, you know? I couldn't get enough of it."

This wasn't making much sense. But then again, New Jerseyans were known for creepier things than fucking in the treetops. I knew. I'd been to their annual food truck festival at the Meadowlands.

"Wow," I said. "I wouldn't have guessed. Windows. Parks. Trees."

"The Jersey Shore was always my favorite, though," she continued. "I'd just bring a lawn chair and watch for hours. I think I learned more at the beach than anywhere else. I've probably taken over a thousand pictures. And I have a bunch of videos on my YouTube channel. It's called Clara's Wildlife. You should check it out. You might learn a thing or two."

Okay, now I was insulted. "I'm thirty years old," I said. "Believe it or not, I already know a thing or two. I actually think of myself as kind of an expert on the subject."

Her face lit up. "Oh my God. Really?"

I shrugged, suddenly bashful. "Really," I said. "Or so I choose to believe. But I guess all men choose to believe that."

"Are you kidding me?" she said. "You're the only man I've met who's even interested."

"Are *you* kidding *me?*" I said. "If there's one thing every man on earth is interested in, it's your area of expertise. You of all people should know that."

"No," she said. "It's the exact opposite. Most men think it's the most ridiculous thing in the world. I must have heard the words 'stop wasting your life' and 'get a real job' about a hundred times."

I didn't reply. Despite the fact that I couldn't wait to get home and check out some of the videos on Clara's Wild Life, I agreed with the hundred or so men who told her she was wasting her life. She was clearly smart enough to succeed in a reputable career field. She could pursue her passion on the side. Why did she need to do it for a living?

"Don't you ever worry?" I said.

"About what?"

"Your heath? Your safety?"

"Not really," she said. "I take all the necessary precautions, and I always use plenty of hand sanitizer when I'm performing fieldwork."

Performing fieldwork. Interesting euphemism. "But is that really enough?" I said. "I mean, with all the germs and diseases out there?"

"Oh, trust me, I always wear latex gloves when I'm making physical contact. But it's more for their sake than for mine. The fact is, they're way more in danger of getting a disease from me than I am from them. One touch from my bare skin, and I could infect an entire population."

You don't realize how important a functioning heart is until you feel yours exploding. "Should I be worried?" I asked. "I touched your bare skin when I lifted your head off the steering wheel this morning."

She evidently thought my concern for my impending death from an STD cocktail was the funniest thing she ever heard, because she started cracking up.

"Don't worry," she said. "I don't need gloves when I'm operating intraspecies. It's only when I work outside my species that I'm a communicable danger. Particularly when I'm collecting stool samples. To get the sample you have to do a scraping in a very sensitive area and it can draw blood."

Explosion number two. Jumping out of a moving car was sounding better by the second. I suddenly had a desperate longing to rewind back to when the most disturbing thing in Clara's world was New Jerseyans fornicating in the canopy while she sat in a beach chair taking videos.

"In retrospect," she continued, "I probably should have worn safety gear when I was on the beach. I'm not kidding when I say I would sit there for three or four hours straight. I can't tell you how many times I got my head pooped on. And knowing what I know now about the communicable hazards of fecal exchange—"

"Can we please pull off at a gas station?" I interrupted. Although I was trying to seem composed, I was about two seconds away from a major coronary event. "I have to use the bathroom."

"Oh, sorry," she said, hitting her right blinker. "I should have asked if you needed to stop. We can get off at the next exit."

CHAPTER 9

CLARA

He liked Ben Harper. He was quick-witted and clever. And he was fascinated by my career, asking question after question. I could barely believe it: I liked Ian and enjoyed his company. And he liked me and enjoyed my company.

And he evidently really, really needed to pee. He was maniacally pulling at the door handle before I even came to a complete stop.

"Take it easy," I said as I put the car into park. "It gets stuck sometimes." I leaned across and grabbed the door handle. "You just have to pull it up a lit—"

I stopped when I saw the look of terror on his face. His back and arms were plastered against the seat in desperate attempt to avoid physical contact with me. "Sorry for disgusting you with my mere existence," I said, sitting up straight. "I promise not to come within two feet of your aura again."

"Thank you," he said.

And just like that, he was an obnoxious jerk again.

"Seriously?" I said. "That's the best you can do?"

"What else do you want?"

"How about instead of a thank-you, you give me an apology?"

"Apology for what?" he said.

"For recoiling just now when I leaned over to open the door. Am I really that repulsive?"

"No," he said. "You're not repulsive. At all. You're really quite attractive. And interesting and fun and clearly very intelligent. Which is why I don't understand your choices. You could do anything you wanted. Why this?"

My heart sank. He was just like all the others. He thought my love of birds and my passion for conservation and ecology were a waste of time, and that devoting my life to preserving endangered species wasn't a "real job."

"I happen to be very proud of what I do. And I'm damned good at it. I've gotten awards."

He looked at me like I was completely delusional. "Who the hell is giving out the awards?"

"The state of Florida, for one."

He just sat there, face blank. Evidently my life's work was such a waste of time that it had rendered him speechless. "They gave you an award?" he finally said. "And that's something you're proud of?"

"I'm proud because I'm providing a very important service. There are a lot of people out there who happen to think I'm making the world a better place to live."

"I'm sure there are," he said. "That's the problem. If it seems like I'm mad, it's because I am. I just don't understand why a woman like you would be proud of selling herself out like she's nothing more than a piece of meat."

"A piece of meat?" I said, completely confused.

I suddenly had a flashback to this morning. I had just woken up and was still disoriented. I saw a stranger at my side and asked him if we'd fornicated. He'd said, *I prefer my women free-of-charge.*

Oh my God. All this time. Recoiling from my touch. Repeatedly using the words "a woman like you."

Listening to me talk about the instructional videos on my YouTube channel.

"Holy shit," I said, aghast. "You think I'm a hooker?"

CHAPTER 10

IAN

She was livid.

"No!" I said. "Not a hooker. What I meant to say was . . . a sex technician?"

"A *what?*"

"Pleasure consultant?"

"Are you kidding me?"

"I'm sorry if I'm not using the politically correct term. And believe me, I'm not some sexist throwback who thinks women don't have the right to choose how they use their own bodies. I respect your choices. But I don't understand them."

"My choice," she said, making air quotes around the word "choice," "is to be a PhD candidate at Columbia University."

I was sure I'd heard her right. But I wasn't sure I believed her. A PhD candidate? "You're serious?"

She grabbed her bag and pulled out her wallet. "You need proof?" she said, throwing a laminated card at me. "There's my campus ID. Read it and weep."

I picked up the card from my lap. Sure enough, it was a Columbia University ID bearing the name "Clara

Zapata." I looked at the picture, then up at my driver. Yep. This was her. Not a sex engineer. Not an orgasmatician. A graduate student.

How the fuck was I going to get myself out of this one? I decided to give *let's just pretend none of this ever happened* a try. "So," I said, "what's your field of study?"

"Get the hell out of my car!"

"Is that a new discipline?" I tried to joke. "I haven't heard of it before."

She wasn't amused. "I'm an ornithologist!"

"Oh my God, are you kidding me?" I cried in sorry attempt to salvage the situation. "I love ornithols!" In reality, I had no idea what an ornithol was, other than OJ Simpson's first name. "Small world, huh?"

She wasn't falling for it. She pulled a hundred-dollar bill out of her wallet, rolled it up, and inserted it into my shirt pocket like a sex-club patron inserting a dollar into a stripper's underwear. "Have the gas station attendant call you an Uber. We're through here."

"Clara, please don't do this. I'm sorry. Really, really sorry."

"I said get out!"

"We're still over a hundred miles from the city! I'll have to pay the driver for the ride there *and* the drive back. It's more than either of us have."

"Not my problem."

"Twelve hundred."

"Twelve hundred what? Blowjobs?"

"Dollars. For the ride."

"I'd rather sell my body for sex," she said. "I remember this one time when I made four hundred dollars just for sitting next to a guy in his car. God knows what I could have made if I'd actually slept with him."

"Come on, Clara—Ms. Zapata—Dr. Zapata?"

"That's 'Bunny Lovemuffin' to you!"

"You're a student and all students need money. So just let me—"

"You're right, I'm a starving student and I desperately need the money, and I'd *still* rather give up twelve hundred easy dollars than spend another minute with you."

"Fifteen hundred," I said. "Cash. That's my final offer."

"It's been real," she said, leaning over me and pushing the passenger door open. "Let's do it again sometime. Ta."

I stepped out of the car, but not without a final plea. "Seventeen hundred?"

She pulled the car door closed with a slam and drove away.

At the edge of the gas station parking lot was a pink Porta John with "Eat my shit, Bertha!" graffitied on the door. I walked over to the bench in front of it and sat down. What the hell was I supposed to do now? The obvious answer was to borrow a phone from the attendant and call my father. But then I imagined explaining the series of stupidities and irresponsible behaviors that had gotten me into this mess in the first place. I'd already gotten a million lectures from him on what a careless failure I was. But now, for the first time ever, Dad would actually be right.

The sound of a car backfiring shook me from my thoughts. Driving back in my direction was Bunny Lovemuffin in the shitmobile. Thank the Lord and the entire host of heaven.

I jumped up and started waving my arms in the air like a shipwrecked sailor who'd just detected a rescue boat on the horizon. Not that Clara actually needed any help spotting me. I was jumping up and down in front of a giant pink toilet with "Eat my shit" spray-painted in purple bubble letters above my head. I was hard to miss.

But as the car careened into the parking lot at about fifty miles an hour, it occurred to me that "hard to miss" might not be the best thing to be right now. But no sooner had the words "vehicular manslaughter" entered my head than the car came to an abrupt halt ten inches from where I stood.

Clara stuck her furious head out the window. "A pleasure consultant? Seriously?"

"I was trying to be polite!" I said in an attempt at self-defense. "Every time you log on to the internet, there's a new word for it. How's a man supposed to keep up?"

"I bet you were pretty eager to log on to my YouTube channel and watch my videos!"

"Not after you said that thing about taking stool samples, I wasn't!"

She pulled her head back into the car and began rolling up her window.

"Clara, let me explain!" I yelled as she put the gear shift into reverse.

"Explain what?" she yelled. "That you thought I went to Florida and won the Investment Ratio of DeNiro War?"

Unless Robert DeNiro had personally declared a war against Florida for misrepresenting its expenditure ratios and conscripted Clara to command his private army, I was pretty sure I'd misheard her.

"Could you repeat that?" I said, gesturing for her to roll down her window.

She opened it just a crack. "You thought I went to Florida and won the Best Fellatio of the Year Award?"

That is what I thought.

"If any state sponsored a yearly fellatio contest, trust me, it would be Florida. Didn't you ever go to Tampa for spring break?"

"I won an award for a lecture I gave at Everglades National Park on the danger of the invasive South American tegu on native amphibians and ground-nesting birds!"

Birds. Now I remembered. Ornithology was the study of birds. "No kidding?" I said, trying once again to get into her good graces. "That sounds fascinating. I'd love to read the transcript sometime."

"Bullshit! Even I was bored!"

There was no point in trying to pretend. "You're right," I said, conceding defeat. "It's bullshit. But can you at least let me try to explain before you drive off and abandon me again?"

"Fine," she said. "Explain. I can't wait to hear your excuse for taking one look at me and assuming I was a hooker."

CHAPTER 11

CLARA

Where the hell did *he* get off being mad at *me?*

As he climbed into the passenger seat, I crossed my arms in front of my chest. I couldn't wait to hear his attempt to justify himself.

"You said, and I quote, 'They're in way more danger of getting a disease from me than I am from them. One touch from my bare skin, and I could infect the entire population.' Those were your exact words. What was I supposed to think?"

"You were supposed to think I was a doctoral candidate at Columbia University!"

"Based on what?" he said. "The fact that you have a bullet hole in your dashboard and woke up on a Saturday morning in a complete stranger's car reeking of vodka, with torn stockings and lipstick smeared all over your face? Or that the first thing you said to me was 'Did we have sex?' followed by 'Thank you for not calling the police?'. I mean, you tell me, Clara, does that sound like an accurate description of a Columbia University student to you?"

"That's the most accurate description of a Columbia University student I've ever heard in my life!" I yelled. "Didn't you go to college?"

He didn't answer. But he didn't need to. We both knew he was right. I did wake up hungover in a complete stranger's car. I did have lipstick all over my face. I did ask him if we had sex, and then thanked him for not reporting me to the police. And to top it all off, when he handed me four hundred bucks, I accepted it without question. And now that I thought about it, I never even mentioned I was a student or an ornithologist. He asked me how I chose my "particular career path" as if he already knew, and I just started rambling on the way I always do whenever someone's stupid enough to say, "tell me more." If I were Ian, I would have been confused, too. *I'd just bring a lawn chair to the beach and sit there and watch for hours. I've taken over a thousand pictures.* Oh my God.

I swallowed. Both my saliva and my pride. The only thing I hated more than being wrong was having to admit it. And I sucked at apologies. So I decided to say I was sorry without saying sorry. "Fine," I said. "I'll drive you back to Manhattan."

"I meant what I said about paying you."

"Forget about it. Free ride for being such a loyal customer."

"Really?" he said.

"Really. This one's on the house."

As I pulled back onto the interstate, I reran the last portion of our increasingly ridiculous conversation in my head.

Loyal customer.

This one's on the house.

Free ride.

Goddammit.

I still sounded like a hooker.

CHAPTER 12

IAN

Since adolescence, I had one question I always asked myself when searching for the solution to a moral dilemma. *What would Dad do?*

And when my soul found the answer, I did the exact opposite.

So if Dad met a beautiful prostitute and treated her like shit for three hours straight, only to find out later that she was a brilliant doctoral candidate, what would he do to make up for it?

Easy question. Nothing. Not a goddamned thing. It would never even occur to him that he'd been hurtful or inappropriate. In fact, he'd be so busy staring at her breasts that he wouldn't even hear "PhD." All he would hear was the voice in his head reciting his favorite mantra. *Boobs . . . boobs . . . boobs-boobs-boobs . . . boobs . . . boobs . . .*

I felt bad about the things I'd said to Clara, and even worse about the things I'd thought. But I was glad that I felt bad. Feelings of remorse meant I still knew right from wrong and was capable of normal human emotions. It meant I'd made it through another day without doing what the world expected me to do: turn into my morally bankrupt father.

I'd learned long ago that the key to maintaining my integrity was vigilance. Whenever I caught myself being selfish or thoughtless or obnoxious, I made a point of nipping my behavior in the bud, rooting it out before it had a chance to blossom into a gigantic asshole tree. I wasn't sure if anything I'd said or done around Clara so far qualified as selfish, but plenty qualified as thoughtless and obnoxious. Which meant it was high time for some bud-nipping.

"I'm sorry," I said.

Clara closed her eyes for a moment, which was more than a little scary since she was driving down I-95 at about sixty miles an hour. But thankfully, she opened them again almost immediately.

"You don't have to apologize," she said, keeping her focus on the road. "I'm not sure why I thought you knew I was an ornithologist. This morning is still kind of hazy to me. But you're right. I asked you if we had sex, I thanked you for not calling the police, and I accepted your money. If I were you, I'm pretty sure I would have thought I was a hooker, too."

"It doesn't matter," I said. "Even if you really were a prostitute, it's no excuse for me being so obnoxious. I sat here talking about respecting your choices, and then treated you like crap because of the choices I thought you made. I don't have the right to treat anyone that way. I don't know what's wrong with me sometimes."

She glanced over at me. "There's nothing wrong with you," she said. "If you want to know the truth, before the little blowup at the gas station, you were starting to grow on me. You actually seem like a pretty good guy." As a small smile crossed her face, she lowered her voice to a whisper. "You didn't hear this from me, but you're fun to talk to."

For a split second, I thought she was just kissing my ass, trying to stroke my ego with false flattery the way most people do when they meet me. But then I remembered that she had no idea who I was. Which meant she had just given me a genuine compliment. The "good guy" who was "fun to talk to" and "kind of growing" on her wasn't the son and only heir of billionaire Daniel Dunning. It was me. Myself. Plain old average non-billionaire Ian Dundunfordsomer.

Something suddenly occurred to me. What if I wanted to contact her again after this ridiculous fiasco was over? What if I wanted to invite her out for a bite to eat, and just talk and hang out and enjoy her company? How would I explain the fake last name? If I couldn't be trusted with information as basic as my own damned name, how could she ever believe anything else I said?

Shit. Now that she was not only not a hooker, but an Ivy League doctoral candidate, did I actively want Clara to like me? And trust me? And want to get together with me after this road trip was over?

And was I imagining it, or was she blushing?

CHAPTER 13

Clara

Was I imagining it, or was I flirting with Ian?

Guys had been hitting on me since I was fourteen, so getting male attention had never exactly been what you'd call a struggle. Which meant flirting was not my thing; I just sat back and let the guys do all the work.

But Ian's only interest in me was as a temporary chauffeur. So I supposed me bluntly telling him that he was growing on me and that he was a good guy was my pathetic attempt to spark his interest while he was my captive audience.

I could feel a flush rising to my cheeks. If I was flirting, I was failing miserably at it. *Don't tell anyone I said this, but you're fun to talk to.* Not exactly a top-ten pickup line.

"So do you drive to work or take the commuter train?" I said, trying to undo my flirt by talking about something banal.

"I work from home," he said.

"Really?" I said with genuine surprise. Him spending his days all alone in that remote little house seemed like a waste of a good personality. "So you're some kind of a hermit?"

He shrugged. "I guess."

"Do you mind if I ask why?"

"I'm self-employed," he said. "I can do everything I need to do from home, so I don't really have any reason to leave."

My curiosity was aroused. "What is it you do?"

"Promise not to yawn?"

"Cross my heart and hope to die."

"Please don't," he said. "The way our luck's been going today, if you cross your heart and hope to die, we'll get hit by a meteor."

I couldn't help but laugh. He really was quite funny. "Then I just promise not to yawn."

"Okay," he said. "But don't say I didn't warn you."

"Tell me already."

"Fine," he said. "I'm a software developer."

I didn't yawn. I was actually quite impressed. His waterfront property suggested he made good money, so I'd assumed he had a job that required brains. But he was also a little dopey. Not unintelligent, mind you, just one of those book smart, life stupid types. The kind who can do calculus in his head and then turn around and lock his keys (and phone and wallet) in his car. Software development—or any job that required logic and critical thinking—was the last thing I would have imagined he did.

"You're serious?" I said.

"Let me guess," he said. "You never would have guessed that I did something that requires me to be logical."

"You've had this conversation with people before?"

"Many times," he said. "Evidently I come off as fairly intelligent on a technical basis but kind of an airhead on a practical one."

"That's not what I was thinking at all," I said, even though that was exactly what I'd been thinking. "It's the way you're dressed that was throwing me off. Button-down shirt. Dress shoes. I just assumed you had a boring office job."

"No," he said. "My work's pretty interesting. And I haven't stepped foot into an office in over five years. Most days in the summer, I don't even bother putting on a shirt. I just sit in front of my computer in a pair of jeans and my bare feet. The only reason I got dressed up last night was because I was supposed to meet my father at some fancy new restaurant. But then he had to work late so we just met at the bar."

I suddenly pictured him sitting in a swivel chair in nothing but a pair of jeans on a hot summer day. Maybe sweating just a little, and taking an ice cube out of his drink and rubbing it down his neck and chest to cool himself down. And then standing up and inserting one thumb under the button of his jeans before pushing his cowboy hat down over his eyes.

Oh my God. I really needed to stop browsing my mother's bookshelves.

"Lucky you," I said. "If you'd gone to the restaurant, you would have ended up driving home in your own air-conditioned car and then gone to sleep at a reasonable hour. And worst of all, you'd be safe and sound in your own house right now enjoying a well-earned Saturday morning off. You're welcome, by the way."

Goddammit. I was flirting again. But either he didn't realize I was flirting, or he realized it and didn't mind, because he was laughing.

"Believe it or not," he said, "I'm kind of enjoying your company, too. Trust me, this is the most interesting Saturday morning I've had in eight months."

"Eight months?" I repeated. "Intriguingly specific. Dare I ask?"

"I don't recommend it."

"Okay, now you have to tell me. What happened eight months ago that could possibly be more interesting than spending the morning with me in my 1999 Cougar?"

He raised an eyebrow. "How much time do you have?"

CHAPTER 14

IAN

I didn't want to tell Clara about Greta.

But then again, I desperately wanted to tell her about Greta. After keeping my feelings to myself for eight months, I wanted to share my heartache with someone who could be trusted not to sell my sob story to the press. But I couldn't tell Clara the full story of my hellish breakup without mentioning my father's money, and the minute she found out who my father was, it was goodbye, Blank Slate, and hello, Mr. Bazillionaire. So I had to be careful with my words. I had to give her the story without divulging all the details—to be honest with her without giving her monetary facts that might overwhelm her moral compass.

"I was engaged," I began carefully. "The short story is that eight months ago I asked for a prenup. When I woke up the next morning, she was gone."

Clara's face was expressionless, her unblinking eyes on the road. I wasn't sure what to make of her sudden silence, but my gut said she thought I got what I deserved for asking the woman I loved for a prenup. Of course, if she knew all the dirty details, she'd know that asking for that prenup had saved me from a loveless marriage and, eventually, a very costly divorce.

"You're very quiet," I said. "Did I say something offens—"

"Was it worth it?" she interrupted.

"Was what worth it?"

"Asking her to sign a prenup? Was it worth losing the woman you loved over?"

"I regretted it at first," I said. "But eventually, yeah, I realized it was worth it. A few months after she left me, she was engaged again. To someone with more money." I very deliberately avoided the word "wealth."

"That doesn't necessarily mean she was a gold digger," she said, her tone more hurt than angry.

"What else would it mean?" I said.

"It means there were only two options for her next boyfriend. Someone who made more money than you or someone who made less. There was a fifty-fifty chance that she'd end up with someone with more. It doesn't mean that money was a deciding factor."

I could see her point. But of course, what she didn't realize was that Greta didn't just dump me for a guy with more money. She dumped me for the *only* guy with more money.

"Let me clarify," I said. "He had a *lot* more money than I did."

She grew silent again. And this time, she stayed silent. I wondered if she'd been engaged once, and if the guy had left her when she refused to sign a prenup. And maybe she had refused for the same reason Greta had pretended to refuse—because she was planning out their happily ever after while he was planning out the divorce.

"Listen," I said, "it's not like I think that the only thing women care about is money—"

"What if you were wrong?" she said.

If only she knew. "I'm pretty sure I wasn't."

"I'm pretty sure you were."

"How could you know that? You never met her."

"I know because if all she cared about was money, she wouldn't have wasted her time on you in the first place."

Wow. I wasn't even sure what she meant by that, but I was grievously insulted.

"Don't get me wrong," she continued. "I've seen where you live and clearly you do well financially. But this is New York. There are a lot of really, really rich men to be found. A genuine gold digger would have set her sights a lot higher."

Wasted her time. Set her sights higher. It was rare that anyone said anything negative about me to my face. People told me what they thought I wanted to hear because they thought there was something to be gained by kissing the ass of Daniel Dunning's son. The end result was that I hadn't been the recipient of an honest opinion since I was thirteen years old. But now that I was with someone who had no reason to lavish me with empty flattery, I was discovering that honest opinions kind of sucked.

"That was a little hurtful," I said. Fuck it. If she was going to be honest, so was I. "I take that back. It was really, really hurtful. I'd go so far as to say it was mean and unnecessary."

"Really?" she said. "Because I was trying to be nice. I just meant that you're a monumental dick for letting her go."

"Using the word 'nice' a little loosely these days, aren't we?" The only time women uttered the word "dick" in my presence was to tell me what a magnificent specimen mine was. It was the one form of empty praise that didn't bother me. And I definitely liked the way Megan and Isla and Greta said it better. They made me feel like the Big Bad Wolf in bed. *Why, Ian, what a monumental dick you have…*

She hit the blinker and pulled off at the next exit.

"I have to pee again," she said. "Sorry that we keep stopping."

She pulled into a gas station and hopped out of the car, leaving me alone to steam. I was officially pissed. Even worse than being called a dick was being wrongfully accused. I was the one who had been madly in love. I was the one who was used and thrown away like a piece of trash. I was the one who had his heart broken. I was the victim, not Greta.

But to be fair to Clara, she didn't know the whole story. And the reason she didn't know the whole story was that I wasn't giving it to her. What right did I have to stew? If I was wrongfully accused, it was because I was a bad witness. Clara was the jury, and she couldn't be expected to hand down a fair verdict based on a half-truth, a missing truth, and everything but the whole truth.

But I had a feeling there was more to her guilty verdict than lack of evidence. Her own bias was playing into her assumption that I was the one in the wrong. She was a little too offended, a little too convinced that Greta was the one whose heart had been smashed to bits.

She returned to the car with two bottled waters and handed one to me.

"So," I said as we pulled back onto the highway, "I take it someone's asked you to sign a prenup?"

She kept her eyes on the road ahead. "What makes you think that?"

"You seemed really upset by my story," I said. "I thought maybe you had some experience in the area."

"I didn't realize I was that obvious."

"It was just a guess."

"Well, it was a good guess," she said. "Yeah, I was engaged. And yeah, he asked for a prenup."

"And I assume you said no?"

"I didn't say no," she said. "But I did ask why."

"And what did he say?"

"Some BS about how his parents were making a big deal out of it, so he just wanted one to get his mom and dad off his case."

"And you didn't believe him?"

"Not for a minute," she said. "His parents were crazy about me. They never would have demanded a prenup."

"So what do you think was the real reason?"

"I don't know," she said, shrugging.

Bullshit. She must have done something to make him think she was after his money. Why else would he feel the need to safeguard it? "You seemed pretty sensitive about me saying Greta was a gold digger. Is that what your fiancé thought you were?"

"No," she said. "Tyler was the spender. He was the one who always wanted more. The only thing we ever really argued about was money, but he was the one always accusing me of being cheap, not the other way around. Trust me, he knew that a gold digger was about the last thing I was."

Based on her mode of transport, it was clear she wasn't a big spender. But why the hell else would a man ask for a prenup? The whole point was to protect your financial assets. There had to be more to the story. And I couldn't help but be curious. Really, really curious.

"You really have no idea why he asked for a prenup?"

"I mean, yeah," she said, hesitant, "I have an idea."

"I told you about Greta. I think it's only fair that you tell me about Tyler."

"You'll think it's stupid," she said. "Or that I'm spoiled or conceited or something."

I already knew she wasn't stupid. And spoiled? By what? A complimentary bullet with every car purchase? "I promise I won't think you're stupid or conceited or spoiled."

She glanced at me. "In that case, can I ask you an awkward question?"

"Sure," I said.

"Do you think I'm pretty?"

I was taken aback. She didn't seem like the kind of person who cared what people thought of her looks. "Yeah," I said, a little embarrassed. "I do."

"And you said that you think women can be gold diggers, right?"

"I didn't mean *all* women. I just meant that there are women out there who only go after men for their money."

"And what if you put the shoe on the other foot? Do you think there are men out there who only go after women for their looks?"

Thanks to Dad, it was the easiest question I'd been asked in ten years. "Yes," I said. "No question."

"Pick up my phone and pull up the camera roll."

I did as told. "Am I looking for anything in particular?" I said as I began scrolling through what seemed like an endless theater of birds.

"Yeah," she said. "When you get past the birds, there are some pictures from a vacation I took last summer. Have a look."

I scrolled through about a thousand pictures before I finally found a batch dated from the end of July. They were mostly taken on beaches and boats, and mostly with Clara wearing sundresses and bikinis.

I stopped on a picture of Clara and another woman standing on a boardwalk, arms around each other's backs. Clara looked pretty damn nice in a strapless sundress. And with her long hair hanging loose and messy over her tanned shoulders, I could reaffirm that she was very attractive.

But she was nothing compared to the other woman. Her companion was absolutely stunning. Busty. Torso like an hourglass. Radiant blue eyes. Full, pouty lips straight out of a lipstick ad. Long, thick brown hair down to her elbows. Cheekbones to die for. She looked a lot like Clara, but a little older. And about ten times as beautiful.

I tried to sound casual. "This person here," I said, holding up the phone for her to see. "You look a lot alike. Is she your sister?"

"No," she said. "She's my mother."

CHAPTER 15

Clara

Mouth agape. No words coming out. Eyes wide and unblinking. The same look everyone wore when they saw my mother for the first time.

"She's forty-nine," I said, answering the question Ian was too dumbstruck to ask. "Those pictures are from her birthday last year. We went to San Diego for a week."

"She's your *mother?*" he said. "How old is she?"

"I just told you, forty-nine."

"And she's your mother?"

"Yes," I said, "she's my mother."

I was used to people going into shock when they realized that the woman who out-beautied me by about a thousand percent was my mom. But I wasn't used to them going into stupid. "In case you're wondering, she's forty-nine. She's my mom, by the way."

He returned his gaze to the phone. Then back to me. Then back to the phone again. Then back to me.

"To answer your next question, yes, my father is the culprit behind my thighs and eyebrows."

"It's not that," he said. "It's just . . . how is it possible to look like that at forty-nine? Has she had work done?"

"Just a tummy tuck from when she dated a plastic surgeon," I said. "The procedure was her Christmas present."

"And that's it? This is really what she looks like?"

"She dyes her hair, if that counts."

"She looks very good for a woman her age. For a woman any age, for that matter. Is she a model or something?"

The traffic was increasing as we approached the city, and I pumped the brakes a little harder than necessary. "Something like that," I said, struggling to maintain a neutral demeanor. I tended to get defensive the minute I suspected someone was about to start judging—or misjudging—my mother, and I could already feel myself getting worked up emotionally.

"What about your dad?" he asked.

"What do you want to know about him?" I said.

"What did he do for a living?"

Ah, there it was, as predictable as time. Ask about the woman's looks. Ask about the man's personality. "From what I gather from my mom," I said, "he stood under bridges and made people answer riddles if they wanted to cross."

He laughed. "So I take it you didn't know him?"

"He was gone before I was even born."

"In that case, you were better off without him. What the hell was a woman like your mother doing with a troll like your father in the first place?"

Yet another question I'd grown accustomed to answering. "Falling in love," I said. "Dreaming of a happy marriage with children and a house with a white picket fence. The same thing as any normal, average-looking person. If you can imagine such a thing."

I regretted my sarcasm as soon as I heard it echoing through the car. But it was incredibly frustrating when people automatically assumed that, because my mother was beautiful, her life was easy and she got everything she ever wanted handed to her on a silver platter when, in fact, the opposite was true.

"I'm sorry," Ian said. "Did I say something wrong?"

As the traffic slowed to ten miles an hour, I hit the blinker and moved into the less-congested middle lane. "Kind of," I said. "But I'm not mad or anything. Everyone does it. Not just men. Women do it, too."

"Women do what?"

"React the way you did when you saw my mother. Ask the same questions."

"Like is she a model and how did she end up with a bum like your father?"

"Yes," I said.

"I just meant that she obviously could have done better."

"Why?"

"Why what?"

"Why is it obvious she could have done better?"

He looked at me like I was crazy for even asking such a stupid question. I was used to that, too.

"Look at her," he said, holding up the phone for me to see like I didn't know what my own mother looked like. "She could have had any man she wanted."

I knew what he meant by "any man she wanted." He meant rich. Because the whole world knew that if a woman was beautiful, she was a shallow, stupid slut who spent her whole life dreaming of marrying a rich man who treated her like a fucking hunting prize to show off to his rich asshole friends. After all, what woman in her right mind would want love and respect when she could have cash instead?

"What she wanted," I said, coming very close to losing my cool, "was a man who loved her regardless of how she looked. But what she got instead was one rich megalomaniac after another parading her around like she was the gold medal in the 'Hottest Girlfriend on Wall Street' competition. She wasn't a prize for some rich bastard to lock up in his trophy case. She was a woman with hopes and dreams and feelings who wanted to be loved for who she was, same as anyone else."

Out of the corner of my eye, I saw Ian look down at his lap, seeming ashamed. That I was *not* used to. No matter how hard I tried to explain my mother's situation, no one ever even tried to understand. If you were a good-looking woman, you were a brat who got everything you wanted. Case closed. Shut up and stop complaining. But Ian? He actually looked kind of sympathetic.

"I'm sorry," I said. "I didn't mean to go off on you like that. I just get upset when I think of all the times my mom was used by men she thought loved her."

He kept his gaze focused on his lap. He looked almost despondent, and I was starting to feel a little guilty for holding him personally responsible for the actions of others.

"You didn't say anything wrong," I said. "Really. You actually seem a lot more understanding than most—"

"So did she finally get smart and start dumping the bastards?" he interrupted.

I was shocked. His tone was tense, even a little angry. I could hardly believe it. He agreed with me. But he probably wouldn't agree with what I was going to say next.

I put the car into park as the traffic came to a complete standstill. “No,” I said, looking over at him. “She finally got smart and started marrying them.”

CHAPTER 16

IAN

Toward the end of his long and illustrious career, Freud observed that the one question he could never answer was: *What do women want?* As a general rule, I wasn't a fan of Freud's penis-centric view of humanity, but at the moment, I kind of agreed with him. Not two minutes ago, Clara had been bemoaning the injustices inflicted upon her mother by trophy-hunting males. And now here she was, telling me that her mother not only sold herself out as a trophy, but was "smart" to do so. *What do women want?*

"So which is it?" I asked.

"Which is what?"

"First you tell me how sad it is that your mother never found true love, but then you tell me she was smart to marry men for their money. So which is it?"

She leaned back in her seat and rubbed her eyes. "It's hard to explain," she said. "To someone who hasn't been there, I mean. My mother didn't sell herself out as a trophy and then expect to be loved for it. She fell in love and then realized she was a trophy. And it's not like it only happened once or twice. It happened so many times that she finally just gave up. She stopped wasting her time looking for love and started giving men what they wanted: a smokin' hot babe they could show off. An adoring female whose sole purpose was to tell them how strong and brilliant and powerful they were and look sexy while doing it. They treated her like a professional ego-stroking service. Why shouldn't she treat them like a professional credit card?"

At last, I was starting to follow. I was starting to follow so well it hurt. The fact was, not only had I "been there," but I'd been thinking along the same lines just the night before. If all a woman was ever going to want me for was money, why shouldn't I expect a pretty face and a hot body in return? If my only options for a life partner were a beautiful woman who didn't love me or an unattractive woman who didn't love me, why shouldn't I go for the beautiful one?

It wasn't what I wanted. Not by a long shot. But the fact was, I understood Clara's mother. Being used and deceived was exhausting, and I got why she finally just threw in the towel and started using men right back. It wasn't that she wanted to be a trophy. It was that she didn't think she had a choice in the matter.

But there was one thing I still didn't understand. "If you think it's okay for a woman to be a gold digger," I said, "why were you so hell-bent on defending Greta when I said all she wanted me for was my money?"

She seemed shocked. "You thought I was defending Greta?"

"I didn't think it," I said. "I heard it with my own ears. Loud and clear. You said I was a monumental dick for assuming Greta was a gold digger. Don't tell me you don't remember it."

"I remember it," she said. "But I wasn't defending Greta. I was defending you."

"Defending me?" I said. "Against what?"

"Yourself. The same way I do when my mother tells me all any man will ever love her for is her appearance."

"You call your mother a monumental dick? To her face?"

"We have a non-traditional relationship," she said. "My point is, you're a dick for selling yourself short. For assuming that all any woman could ever love you for is your money."

"Why do you assume it's an assumption?"

"Because gold diggers look for men who are just as shallow as they are. My mother's dated a lot of rich men, and you're nothing like them. They're shallow. They're selfish. They're egotistical. You're not any of those. You're down-to-earth. You're smart and funny, and the more time I spend with you, the more I like you. All I'm saying is, I can definitely see where a woman would take it a step further and fall in love with you. So you're a dick for shortchanging yourself and refusing to accept the fact that *maybe*, just maybe, a woman could see you as more than a pot of gold. You're a good guy and a nice person. So stop fighting it and start accepting it, Ian. You're worth loving."

CHAPTER 17

CLARA

He wasn't looking at me. He was staring straight ahead, his expression tense. Whatever it was I'd said that upset him, I regretted saying it.

"I'm sorry," I said. "I didn't mean to ramble. Forget everything I just said."

"It's okay," he said.

But clearly it wasn't okay. I'd meant it when I told him that the more time I spent with him, the more I liked him. We'd been getting along. We'd been talking and joking and laughing and enjoying each other's company. And then I had to go and open my big mouth. What the hell did I know, anyway? Maybe this Greta character really was a gold digger, one who was new to the club and didn't realize that, in order for the trophy marriage to work, she needed to find an actual trophy hunter. You can't make just any man not love you for who you are. You have to find a man who *wants* to not love you, who gives as little a shit about you as you give about him. And only when you've found a man as shallow and selfish as you are will you at last feel the true joy of being bound for eternity—eternity here being defined as an average of thirty-eight months—to someone who deserves not even an ounce of your respect. Only then will you experience the true magic of not being remotely in love with the inflation-adjusted annuity you fuck every Tuesday and Friday.

I had misjudged Ian. No one had ever shown an ounce of compassion when I talked about how my mother had been used by men. Until Ian. He understood. He sympathized. Looking at him now, I could see that he wore his heart on his sleeve. You could see the vulnerability from a mile away. Mining him for gold would be like hunting for cows in a barn. He was what the more heartless women in my mother's line of work called "ripe for the picking." So yeah, maybe Greta really was a gold digger.

I should have known better than to pass judgment. After all, hadn't I just been dumped by a man whose love for me was contingent upon me keeping my girlish figure? Who was I to say that Greta's love for Ian wasn't contingent upon him bringing in a fat paycheck? Simply stated, I suspected that Ian was to Greta what I was to Tyler. A target. A fool. Tyler was a trophy hunter, but I wasn't a trophy. Greta was a gold digger, but Ian wasn't a mine.

Which meant Ian and I were two birds of a feather. A limp, broken feather. We'd both been played. We'd both been made fools of. We'd both had our hearts broken.

"Ian?" I said.

"Hm?" he responded.

"What you said about Greta being a gold digger?"

"Yeah?"

"I believe you."

CHAPTER 18

IAN

She was apologizing.

Maybe.

Or maybe not. All I knew for sure was that she thought I was mad or hurt or insulted. I wasn't. I was just flustered. And evidently doing a very bad job of hiding it.

I looked out the passenger-side window to hide whatever pathetic look I had on my face. I'd been told by many, many people that I wore my heart on my sleeve. And at this particular moment, my heart was more than on my sleeve. It was in my stomach. It was in my throat. It was in my freaking eyeballs. Seriously. My left eyelid had a pulse.

"If you're apologizing, there's no need," I said. "I wasn't offended."

"Still," she said, "I shouldn't have contradicted you when you said Greta was only after your money. I wasn't there. I didn't know her. It was just hard for me to imagine someone only wanting you for your money when you obviously have so much more to offer. I mean, even if Greta started out as a gold digger, I feel like she would have fallen in love with you by accident. Like she wouldn't have been able to help herself."

My heart was now pounding in parts of my body I didn't even know had veins. My left ass cheek. My earlobes. I had to get it under control. There was only so long I could pretend to be fascinated with the green Buick in the next lane.

"Do you believe me when I say that I believe you?" she asked, unwilling to let it go.

While I wasn't ready to look her in the eyes, I did manage to bring my gaze to the dashboard. "Yes," I said.

"And you're okay?"

"I'm fine," I said, forcing myself to believe it. "Really."

"Are you sure? Because it seems like maybe you're not really over her yet."

I took one last deep breath. "I just have the occasional flashback, that's all. Get a little emotional."

It was a lie. I wasn't in love with Greta anymore. But I'd rather Clara think I was obsessing over my broken engagement than let her know the real reason I was so agitated.

"What about you?" I said, deliberately changing the subject. "Do you ever have Tyler flashbacks?"

"Yeah," she said. "A lot, actually. I don't know why, though. I know he was a jerk and I'm better off without him. I'm just having a hard time moving on, I guess."

"You'll get there," I said. "You'll see. It's just not as logical a process as you'd like it to be. Even when you know that you're better off without someone, it takes a while for your heart to catch up with your brain."

She smiled forlornly. "Define 'a while.'"

"For me it took about five months to accept it and really start moving on. How long has it been since Tyler broke up with you?"

"Two weeks," she said.

"Oh," I said, shocked. For some reason, I'd imagined her breakup was a few months in the past. "I had no idea it was so recent. Do you mind if I ask how it happened?"

She smiled a weak smile. "Darn," she said jokingly. "Did I accidently leave out the best part?"

"Please don't tell me he did it in a restaurant so that you wouldn't make a scene or something cliché like that."

"Better," she said. "He sent me a text while I was at the bridal shop getting my dress refitted to accommodate my extra weight." She pinched the few inches of flesh at her waistline. "Meet pounds one through fifteen. They're the reason he broke off the engagement."

It took me a moment to take it in. "You're serious?" I said, making sure she wasn't just messing with me. "He broke up with you over your weight?"

"Yes," she said.

"By text?"

"Yes."

"While you were at the bridal shop?"

"Yes."

Holy shit. My breakup was officially out-awfuled. By leaps and bounds. Comparatively speaking, Greta picking up and leaving in the middle of the night without a goodbye seemed like an act of angelic mercy. What Clara had been through was absolutely heartbreaking. I pictured her standing there in her wedding dress in front of a three-way mirror, a seamstress with a tape measure telling her to tuck in her tummy and stand up straight while her mother and maid of honor sat on the sidelines telling her what a beautiful bride she was going to be. And then a text tone pinging. And then her looking down at her phone. And then her whole world crashing down.

"I don't know what to say, Clara." And I didn't. What do you say to someone whose heartbreak was served with a heaping side of public humiliation? "That must have been awful."

It was then that something occurred to me. Brides start shopping for their wedding dress about five minutes after the proposal, but they wait until the last possible minute to have their final alterations done. "So," I said, a little afraid to hear the answer to the question I was about to ask, "when was the wedding supposed to be?"

It looked like her hands were shaking on the steering wheel. Then she uttered just one word:

"Tomorrow."

CHAPTER 19

CLARA

In my younger and more vulnerable years, my mother gave me some advice that I've been turning over in my mind ever since.

Don't be an asshole.

I never knew if Mom came up with that one on her own or if she stole it from the Annals of Confucius. But I do know that it's the best piece of advice anyone has ever given me. I've always thought of it as my family's secular version of *What Would Jesus Do?* What would an asshole do? Figure it out, and then don't do it. If you're not in the mood to do the dishes, don't be an asshole and leave your mess for someone else to clean up. If someone is a dick to you on the playground (Mom's actual words, by the way), don't be an asshole by pushing them off the swing. And if a guy breaks your heart? Don't be an asshole and let today's sadness dictate the next six months of your life.

That last piece wasn't advice. It was a household rule. Growing up, anytime something really bad happened, I had exactly two days to wallow in self-pity. When the forty-eight-hour timer went off, I had to get off my sorry ass (again, Mom's actual words), get back on my feet, and move the hell on.

I admit that I didn't always stop wallowing after two days. But I did learn to get back on my feet no matter how miserable I felt. The rule was, if you insisted on feeling sorry for yourself beyond the forty-eight-hour mark, fake it. Put on a brave face and soldier on.

I know. It sounds harsh. And it is. The thing is, it works. This might surprise every psychologist and school counselor in the history of earth, but faking it is a miracle cure. Acting outwardly strong produces actual inner strength. Putting on a brave face builds a strong heart. It's the "soldiering through" that makes you a soldier. It's like dressing for the job you want and not the job you have. Putting on a suit does more than just make you look like an executive—it makes you feel like one. And once you start feeling like one, you start thinking and behaving like one. It's playacting, but it's playing the part that turns you into a player.

Thanks to Mom forcing me to pretend to be a soldier, I became one. Your father abandoned you? March on. Your stepfather walked out on you the day after you asked him if you could call him Dad? March on. Your best friend slept with your boyfriend? March on.

But there's a big difference between being a soldier and being an impenetrable fortress. Sometimes something's so bad you can barely walk, let alone march. Even Mom knew that. And when I was in the bridal shop holding up the breakup text for her to read, the first thing she did was hug me. And then she whispered words I never thought I would hear coming from her lips: "You can take more than two days for this one."

It was the first time I'd cried in my mother's arms since my cat got hit by a car in the second grade. Two full decades without breaking down in front of Sergeant Badass. But she let me have my cry that day. And trust me, it was a doozy. And it didn't exactly end in the bridal shop, either. I cried all the way home. I cried walking up the six flights of stairs to my apartment. I cried myself to sleep that night, and the next morning I cried myself awake. And the day after that, I cried as I sat behind the bathroom door listening to my mother calling the church and the caterers and the wedding guests with the news that they could take Sunday, May 6th off.

But the day after that was Monday. My forty-eight hours were up. It didn't matter that Sergeant Sara "Deal With It" Zapata had given me official orders to take more than two days off. She had trained her little soldier too well, and at nine o'clock Monday morning, I was standing dry-eyed in front of twenty college freshman delivering practice questions for the Biology 101 final. And so I had continued, day after day, night after night, a brave soldier fighting a war against her own emotions, a careful surgeon sewing together the pieces of her own broken heart.

The problem was, it was all a front. For two weeks, I had been pretending to be fine. For two weeks, I'd been waiting for my outward appearance of bravery and strength to mold my inside emotions into conformity. Day after day, I'd soldiered on, believing that any minute, Tyler would become a remnant from my past and the sadness and humiliation and heartbreak would all be behind me.

But it wasn't. For the first time, faking it wasn't working.

And I knew why.

Because you can't leave behind a past that hasn't happened yet. The worst was still ahead of me. Thirty hours from now, I was supposed to be walking down the aisle in my waist-extended white dress toward a teary-eyed man in a tuxedo who had never looked so handsome. Thirty-five hours from now, we were supposed to be dancing the first dance of our married lives under the full moon. And forty-eight hours from now, we were supposed to be snuggled side-by-side in airplane seats as we flew off to Cancun for the most romantic week of our lives.

I could get over the past. But I couldn't get over the future. I still had to survive my canceled wedding day. I still had to survive the honeyless week of my honeymoon. And I had to do it all knowing there were three parents, five bridesmaids, four groomsmen, and over fifty guests thinking, *Poor Clara. Poor, pathetic, one-hundred-and-thirty-seven-pound, thirty-three-inch-waist Clara. I wonder how many chocolate eclairs it will take her to get over this one.*

"Hey," a quiet voice said.

For a moment there, I'd almost forgotten I had a guest in my passenger seat. But there he was, sitting beside me.

"Sorry," I said. "I think I got a little distracted."

"I can drive for a while," he said. "Take a little break. Have a nap if you want."

"I don't need to rest," I said, feigning a smile. "I slept like a drunken baby last night. I actually took this spontaneous camping trip—"

"Clara?"

I looked over to find his expression was dead serious.

"What?" I asked.

"You've been taking care of me all morning. Let me take care of you for a while. I'll drive."

I felt like I was about to cry. But this time, it was not from sadness. It was from gratitude, triggered by the sound of the words *let me take care of you*. No man had ever said that to me before; at the moment, it sounded better than a heartfelt *I love you*.

The traffic was at a dead halt, and Ian got out of the car and walked around the back to the driver's side. "Scoot over," he said as he opened the door. "You ride shotgun."

I sniffled, fighting off a tear. "I appreciate this, Ian," I said as I climbed over the console.

He slid into the driver's seat.

"What are those?" he asked, pointing to the back seat.

"What are what?"

"Those boxes in the back. I just noticed them."

Crap. I'd completely forgotten about my six boxes of sappy heart-shaped wedding cupcakes. I'd just admitted to Ian that I'd more or less been left at the altar, and I wasn't in the mood to humiliate myself any further. So I decided to make light of it. "Are you hungry for lunch yet?"

"I am, actually," he said. "Are those sandwiches?"

"Worse," I said. "Wedding cake." I reached into the back and grabbed one of the boxes. Untaping the sides, I angled it so that Ian couldn't see inside.

"What are you doing?" he said.

"Finding the perfect lunch for you."

I scanned the cupcakes. *Love U*. No. *Soul M8*. Not quite. *PLZ Me*. Wouldn't mind, but not in the middle of a traffic jam in broad daylight.

At last, I spotted one that perfectly captured what I was feeling. I pulled it out of the box and handed it to him.

A smile crossed his face as he read: *U R Sweet.*

He took a bite as he gestured for me to hand him the box.

When I passed it over, he angled it so I couldn't see inside. I couldn't help but notice that he was starting to look pretty handsome. A part of me hoped he was going to find a rogue cupcake with *Can I Fondle U* or *How Bout a QuikE* on it.

But when he finally picked one out, he didn't immediately hand it to me. Instead, he carefully pulled off the white letters and dropped them into the box. He then grabbed a bobby pin from the console tray, straightened it into a writing utensil, and started engraving.

A few moments later, he handed me the cupcake.

I M HappE

I smiled. As I took my first bite of my *HappE* cupcake, I grabbed another from the box, pulled the lettering off, and engraved it with a question.

Y?

He took a bite while he engraved another cupcake. He handed it to me.

Bcuz I Found U

I giggled like a lovesick schoolgirl as I engraved his next cupcake.

I M LuckE

Y?

Bcuz U Found Me

His final cake message took an extremely long time to engrave, and when he finally handed it to me, the lettering was so small I could barely read it.

If We Keep ComUnic8ing by Cake, I M Going 2 B Sick

With a mouthful of cake, I giggled again, and handed him my last cake-o-gram.

Me 2

Eating these sweet feelings was much more satisfying than eating my bitter feelings for Tyler, and I enjoyed my three lunch cupcakes much more than my five breakfast ones. My hand-engraved frosting messages to Ian weren't empty flattery. I *was* lucky. Without him to keep me company, today would have been nothing short of an emotional nightmare.

"These are really good," he said as he took a bite of the *Me 2* cupcake. "How many do you have left?"

"About fifty," I said as I swallowed my last bite. "Are you ready for dinner yet? You'll never guess what's on the menu."

He laughed, almost choking on his last bit of cake. "Don't tempt the evil spirits," he said, pointing to the still unmoving traffic ahead of us, "or we might just end up spending the night here."

I felt a tingling in my fingers and a hollowness in the pit of my overstuffed stomach. I'd been around long enough to know what it was. It was attraction. Ian had said the thing about tempting the evil spirits as a joke, but the truth was, I wouldn't mind spending the night with him. And waking up with him. And then spending another day with him. And most importantly, eating more cupcakes. With or without him.

I had another feeling, this one not so strange. Covering my mouth, I yawned. It had been a long, emotionally exhausting two weeks, and for the first time since that day at the bridal shop, I felt capable of actual, uninterrupted, non-alcohol-induced sleep. "Did you mean what you said about taking a nap?" I asked as another yawn escaped.

"If I had to guess, it'll be at least another two hours before we get to Midtown," he said. "May as well close your eyes and rest."

Rest. What a lovely word. I'd been neck-deep in the trenches for two weeks now, no other soldiers at my flank. But suddenly there was a man at my side offering to shoulder my burden, telling me the hard work of grieving was on hiatus. I could stop fighting for a few hours, because he was going to take care of me.

On any other day, under any other circumstances, I would have been reluctant to fall asleep at the side of a relative stranger. But for whatever reason, I trusted Ian. Maybe it was the gentle tenor of his voice or the softness in his expression, but I believed the only motive behind his kindness was compassion. He wasn't faking being nice in hopes of getting laid.

He was, however, some kind of hypnotist, because before I knew it, I lapsed into a deep, peaceful, and welcome sleep.

CHAPTER 20

IAN

Whatever had been holding up the traffic subsided, and I was finally driving at a full sixty miles an hour on the southbound Cross Bronx Expressway toward Manhattan. But despite the speed, I kept glancing over at Clara. I couldn't help it. If she was pretty when she was awake, she was enchanting when asleep. The word that kept popping into my head was "cuddlable." I kept imagining her long hair spilling over a pillow, a blanket pulled up just high enough to cover her breasts but reveal her bare shoulders. It was a down pillow, it was a blue blanket. It was my bed back home in Connecticut. And it was the night after she received the breakup text. I wished I'd known her then.

Not because I wished I could have been the lucky recipient of an easy rebound lay. I just wished I could have been there for her. I remembered that first night after Greta left, how incredibly painful it had been to sleep in the bed alone. I had never craved a woman's body so badly in my whole life, but the craving had nothing to do with sex. For the first time, I had understood why long-married people referred to their partners as their "other half." Greta leaving felt like an amputation, like half of me was missing. And the only thing that could make me whole again was the warm body of a loving woman tangled up with mine.

I ended up sleeping on the couch for the next two months. I even moved the dresser into the hallway so I wouldn't have to step foot in the bedroom. I eventually moved the mattress into the living room, and then finally threw out the old mattress and bought a new one. When four full months had passed and the pain still hadn't subsided, I sold my condo and everything in it and moved to my weekend house in Connecticut. It ended up being the cure I needed. Five months after the breakup, I was finally on the road to recovery.

But only because I had the financial means to leave it all behind. Clara, on the other hand, probably couldn't have afforded a cheap hotel room after Tyler dumped her. But if she had known me then, she could have called and said, *Come find me, I can't survive this on my own.* And I could have hurried to her side and been the warm body to comfort her that night, and the night after that, and the night after that, and for as many nights as it took for her to accept the end and move on.

Any doubt that I was developing a crush on Clara was erased as soon as she handed me the *UR Sweet* cake. I had to be careful. I had a long history of falling head over heels the minute I felt even the tiniest bit of camaraderie with a woman, and every time, it ended with me realizing that the person I'd fallen madly in love with felt not a genuine ounce of real love for me in return.

But there was one big difference between Clara and Megan/Ilsa/Greta: Clara still had no idea who I was. Our initial meeting had been the product of pure—albeit bizarre—serendipity. The other three women had known exactly who I was, and our "accidental" first meetings were anything but. Megan took out a loan so she could rent an apartment in my building. Ilsa crashed into my parked car so she could leave her name and phone number on my windshield. And Greta? She took the cake. After the breakup, her estranged stepbrother—who made no secret of hating her guts—confided in me that she'd not only been targeting me for years before we met, she'd run for the Special Ed counsel for the specific purpose of getting herself invited to my family's charity banquets. She knew my habits, she tracked my movements. Our 'accidental' meeting was years in the making.

Clara, on the other hand? I felt confident that breaking into my car, ripping her stockings, smearing lipstick all over her face and passing out stinking drunk in my driver's seat wasn't a meticulously planned scheme to make me fall in love with her. Furthermore, I was pretty sure I wasn't going to be saying *You had me at 'monumental dick'* to her anytime soon. If all this was part of her giant plan to seduce me, her seduction skills sucked ass.

And yet here I was, unmistakably smitten. And about two heartbeats away from killing us both in a distracted driving incident.

With great effort, I removed my eyes from Clara and refocused on the road. The Cross Bronx Expressway was no place for daydreaming. Every minute was rush hour, every merge lane and off-ramp a fatal crash waiting to happen. So it was probably a terrible idea to drive it with the world's most beautiful twenty-eight-year-old ornithologist sleeping in the seat beside me.

At last, I reached 63rd Street. About halfway down the block, I saw my car. In a stroke of improbable luck, the very same space Clara had vacated at six o'clock was empty. And in a stroke of astronomical luck, I parallel parked her car without dinging or damaging any other cars. Or storefronts. Or passersby.

When I turned off the engine, Clara shifted. Rubbing her eyes, she looked over at me, confused.

"Why are we stopping?" she said in a sleepy voice.

"We're back," I said.

She propped herself up on her elbows and looked out the front window.

"Is this the same parking spot from this morning?"

"The very same."

She stretched, then rubbed her eyes again. "Well," she said as she returned her seat to the upright position, "I guess this is it."

I felt a pang. *This is it.* As in *goodbye.* I had figured we would spend a little time together after we got to Manhattan, maybe have a real lunch or at least go for a coffee. But apparently not. She was ready to move on.

"Yep," I said, feigning cheerfulness. "This is it. You finally get me out of your life."

"I'm pretty sure you're the one who should rejoice," she said. "If I recall correctly, I was the one who got you into this mess in the first place."

"As messes go," I said, "it was a fun one. Kind of like playing in the mud when you're a little kid." God, what a sorry attempt to draw out a conversation. *Spending time with you is like rolling around in the mud like a pig.* "Like kids playing outside, I mean. Carefree or whatever. I didn't literally mean playing in the—"

"Ian?" she interrupted.

"Yeah?"

"I literally spend about forty days a year wading through mud bogs cleaning filth-covered waterfowl. I wasn't offended."

"Oh," I said. "Ornithologist. Right."

She nodded. I nodded. It appeared that we had run out of things to say.

Which meant this was it. It was over.

It was time to let her go.

CHAPTER 21

Clara

I waited for him to say more. He wasn't going to let it end like this, was he? We'd fought. We'd laughed. One of us had almost cried. We'd shared the most intimate details of our breakups. I told him he was sweet and he told me I made him happy. Surely I wasn't the only one feeling it. This was more than just friendship, wasn't it?

Apparently not. To Ian, at least. Without another word, he handed me my car keys, then stepped out into the street. A moment later, he opened my car door, and I stepped out.

"Well," I said as we stood face to face on the sidewalk, "I won't be forgetting you anytime soon, Ian. It's been an adventure."

"That it has. I'm pretty sure I won't be forgetting you anytime soon either, Clara."

Silence followed. Neither of us moved.

Not really knowing what else to do, I extended my right hand for a formal goodbye shake.

His hand grasped mine, and we shook. And then shook again. And then we just kept shaking.

It was a little weird.

"What the hell," he finally said, letting go. "Come here." He opened up his arms, and I accepted his embrace. There was no shyness or awkwardness. Ian was holding me. I was holding him. Our embrace was the most natural thing in the world. I didn't want it to end.

And it didn't. We stood there, our arms around each other, for I don't know how long. If there were other people on the sidewalk, I wasn't aware of them. All I was aware of was how nicely my head fit between his head and shoulder, how strongly his heart was beating. He squeezed me tighter. I returned the favor. This was no buddy hug. This was two people who didn't want to let each other go.

I felt his warm breath against my ear. "Before you go," he whispered, "can I tell you something? Something you might not want to hear?"

My body froze, my mind going into emotional arrest. The last thing a man had said to me that I didn't want to hear was *U R 2 Fat 2 MarrE.* My ego had been through enough these last few weeks. I didn't even want to venture a guess at what was wrong with me this time.

If Ian wasn't feeling what I was feeling, I didn't want to stick around any longer. I'd just make a fool of myself. Again.

I decided to cut my losses. I wanted to remember Ian as someone who liked me. I wanted my memory of our time together to be a happy one, not one that ended with a recommendation that I take it easy on the cupcakes if I wanted my next engagement to work out. So instead of answering him, I used my never-fail excuse for getting out of an awkward situation.

"Ian?" I said, my arms still around him.

"Hm?" he said.

"I really need to pee."

CHAPTER 22

IAN

In terms of parting words, it wasn't exactly *ET* or *Casablanca.*

I watched her backside disappear into the crowd of pedestrians as she headed to a bathroom and out of my life forever. I cursed myself for my stupidity. Our embrace had been the real deal. I was sure she could feel my heart pounding, and I hadn't imagined her whole body shivering when I pressed my lips to her ear. It had seemed to me that we were admitting our feelings for one another without uttering a word. It was a genuine moment, one that might have led to a kiss and then a romance and then a full-fledged love story.

But then I had to go and open my big mouth. Women had started throwing themselves at me when I was a teenager, so I'd never really had to come up with a signature pickup line or even learn how to talk to the opposite sex. No one was interested in me for my conversational skills. But I'd wanted to say something meaningful to Clara, something like: "Somewhere out there is a man who wants to love you. I promise."

But in retrospect, I probably shouldn't have prefaced it with *Can I tell you something you won't want to hear?* I wondered what it was she imagined I was about to say. Did she think I was going to tell her to lay off the sweets if she wanted her next engagement to work out? Or that her career was a waste of time and she should get a real job? Or some other self-esteem damaging commentary that she'd heard from other guys? God, why couldn't I just have gone with a run-of-the-mill *I wouldn't mind seeing you again* or *Why don't we swap phone numbers just for laughs*? She might still be standing here in my arms. We might even be kissing.

I had a choice to make. Either cut my losses by driving away, or wait around for her to return and risk being rejected. It took me all of about two seconds to decide: I was staying put. If there was even a one-percent chance that Clara was feeling the same way about me as I was about her, it was worth risking rejection. She and I had connected, I was sure of it. And for once in my miserable life, it was real. A woman can fake an orgasm (don't ask me how I know that) but she can't fake a pounding heart. She can fake a sigh, but she can't make her whole body shiver. I didn't think she was madly in love with me, but she felt something. I wasn't going to turn and walk away just because I'd spoken a few poorly chosen words.

Pulling my spare key from my pocket, I pressed the unlock button and climbed into my car. There were now three parking tickets on my windshield, but I didn't care. All I cared about was Clara. She had to return eventually, and I would wait for as long as it took.

Which, knowing the New York City public toilet situation, was going to be a while.

In the meantime, I decided I'd listen to a little music. I started searching for my phone. It wasn't on the passenger seat, where I thought I'd left it. I bent over to look under the seat. Not there, either. It was when I was sitting back up that I noticed something.

A bird-shaped keychain.

For the love of God. Three hundred miles round trip. Six hours in total. Anger, laughter, tears, windshield theft, cupcakes, and Porta Johns galore. What was it all for?

It was for a spare key. A spare key that was good for shit.

Clara's keys were still stuck in my ignition.

I had just dropped my idiot head onto the steering wheel when I heard my phone ping from inside my glove box.

Opening it, I grabbed my phone. On the screen was a message that said "16 new notifications." I was shocked. While I got plenty of texts during the workweek, my Saturdays and Sundays were pretty quiet. So imagine my surprise when my phone pinged again a moment later. And then a third time.

Gran. That had to be it. She'd been in the hospital for a week and I hadn't even visited her yet. And now she was dead and her only grandson had let her die alone. Panicked, I opened the most recent message. It wasn't the hospital telling me Gran had died of loneliness and it was all my fault. It was from a college buddy I hadn't spoken to in over a year.

> *Holy shit man your old man's going to flip. I feel for you, good luck, buddy*

What the . . .?

I pulled up the next message. It was from a douchebag programming colleague whom I'd specifically instructed never to contact me if it wasn't a coding emergency.

Nice, dude. Worth every penny if you ask me

Why were people sending me these cryptic texts? The next was from a number I didn't even recognize.

Ian I'll do you for free!

There was a link, and I stupidly clicked on it. It was a naked selfie of a woman I'd never seen before and never wanted to see again, naked or otherwise.

I read the next text. It was from Dad.

A hotel, Dummy. She books a room. You book a room an hour later. Then you go to her room instead of yours and no one's the wiser. Did that 100K a year prep school I sent you to teach you no life skills?

Dad's bizarre message, like the one before it, had a link. I clicked on it, desperately hoping it wasn't another naked selfie.

It wasn't a naked selfie. It was worse. It was a headline:

Ian Dunning Caught Red-Handed with Prostitute!

Beneath the headline was a picture of me in my car. Clara was standing outside the door in her tight red shirt, torn stockings, and five-inch heels, looking very much like the drunken prostitute I'd first imagined her to be.

And I was sitting in the driver's seat handing her cash out the window.

Shiittt!

I heard a loud knock. I looked over to see Clara standing outside my passenger side door, frantically gesturing for me to open it.

"Ian," she cried, "open up! I just peed on something!"

Just this once, I hoped I was hearing her right. I would much rather listen to her tell me about how she'd just peed on a fire hydrant than hear what she'd have to say if she saw our picture on the internet.

I had to think fast. But I had never been what you'd call cool under pressure. And at the moment, I was pretty sure I was having a full-fledged anxiety attack.

Clara, on the other hand, had never looked happier. Her smile stretched from ear to ear and she was jumping up and down like a kid on Christmas morning. It could only mean one thing: she hadn't seen the headlines yet.

She reached for the door handle. In a panic, I slapped the lock button so she couldn't get in. Except that the door was already locked, so what I actually did was unlock it for her.

At the sound of the click, she opened the door and jumped into my car with what my father's kind would call "irrational exuberance."

"Did you hear me?" she said. "I said I just realized something!"

"Fanks!" I yelled. It was a panicked combination of "fine" and "thanks," neither of which were an appropriate response to *I just realized something.*

"My keys are still stuck in your ignition," she said, that huge smile still glued to her face. "How are you going to get home?"

"Sure!"

"Is something wrong?" she said, her smile disappearing. "You're not making any sense."

"Fine!" I shouted. "Everything's going to be fine!"

Her phone pinged. "Just a minute," she said, grabbing her purse. "Someone keeps texting me. It might be an emergency."

She reached into her bag.

"Don't look at that!" I said.

She frowned at me. "What's going on? You're starting to scare me."

I grabbed her wrist. "Please believe me when I say I'm sorry, Clara. I'm so, so sorry."

"Ian, what the hell is going on? Why are you apologizing?"

Her phone pinged again. There was no point in delaying it any further. It was in God's hands now.

I let go of her wrist and leaned back in my seat. "I'm apologizing for what you're about to see on your phone."

CHAPTER 23

Clara

It's funny, you think the term "two-dollar whore" is just an expression until you see it printed out in red capital letters above a picture of yourself in fishnet stockings and five-inch heels accepting two singles from a male hand protruding from a tinted car window.

"Oh my God!" I said. Or bellowed. Or screamed. I can't remember exactly. Those first ten seconds are still kind of a blur.

"Clara," Ian pleaded, "please let me explain."

My phone pinged again. I opened the goddamned text. It was from my acronym-loving maid of honor, Janie.

> *OMG are you OK? IDK why you'd do something like this but call me ASAP*

I moved on to the next text. It was from my thesis advisor at Columbia.

> *I know it's been rough but you don't need to do this. Call me, please. I'm here for you*

Holy shit. There were still eight messages left to go. How many people had seen the picture?

I checked the next text, from one of the executive directors at Eco-Justice.

> *You should know this will reflect very poorly on the organization*

I scrolled to the next text. It was from Tyler.

> *If you'd bothered to dress like this for me once in a while, maybe we'd still be together*

"Sonofabitch!" I screamed.

"Clara, please—"

"Who the hell are you?" I shouted, holding my phone in front of his face so he could read the headline attached to the text Tyler had sent me.

> *Ian Dunning Rents Two-Dollar Whore!*

"I'm nobody," he said. "Really. I'm just Ian—"

"Dunning," I practically screamed. "I can read. Why the hell did you give me a fake last name and why are the paparazzi following you around taking pictures of you?"

His face was crimson. "I'm kind of a celebrity," he said. "An unwilling one, I swear. And you didn't seem to know who I was when you woke up this morning, so when you asked me my name, I just—"

My phone rang. I looked at the screen.

It was Mom. I was in trouble.

Reluctantly, I hit the green answer button and held the phone up to my ear. "Mommy?"

"Are you fucking kidding me?"

Mommy was not happy.

"Mom, I swear it's not what it looks like."

"Was I a good mother, Clara?" she said. "Did I not teach you good from bad and right from wrong?"

"Of course you did," I said. "You know how much I respect—"

"Then remind me what I've spent the last twenty-eight years of my life teaching you."

I turned my head to the window, keeping my voice low. "Don't be an asshole," I whispered.

"That's right!" Mom yelled. "Don't be an asshole! So you tell me, what kind of asshole only charges two dollars for her services?"

"If you would just let me ex—"

"If I've told you once, I've told you a million times. Not a penny less than five thousand a night. And that's the low end of the pay scale. I've made more than that in a half hour."

I jumped out of the car and slammed the door behind me, hoping Ian hadn't heard any of what my mother had just said. All I'd told him so far was that she'd once been a career trophy wife. I hadn't told him about the extremely lucrative freelance enterprise she'd been engaging in since her last divorce.

"Will you just listen to me for a minute?" I said as I scurried away from Ian's car.

"Listen to what?" she said. "This is Ian Dunning! You could have easily charged ten thousand. If he'd become a regular client, you could have made your entire living off of him."

"He's not a client because I'm not a prosti—"

"You're the one who's supposed to be so smart!" Mom said without letting me finish. "Do the math. You service the guy twice a month at ten thousand a pop, that's almost a quarter mill a year. It would have left you with all the time in the world to wash ducks in Palmolive."

"It's Dawn, because it has a grease cutter, and would someone please tell me who the fuck Ian Dunning is already?"

"He's your client from last night!"

"I know who he is technically!" I shouted. "I mean who is he that he's making headlines? Is he some movie star I've never heard of or something?"

"Are you serious?"

"Yes, I'm serious."

"He's the son of Daniel Dunning. How can you not know that?"

"The son of *who?"*

"Daniel Dunning. The billionaire. You should know that."

"How the hell would I know some billionaire?"

"Ian's his only son. He stands to inherit everything." She went silent for a moment. "Actually, now that I think of it, you should keep giving it to him for free. He's worth way more to you as an ex-husband than as a client. Did you by any chance get his number?"

"For the last time," I yelled aloud in the open street, "he's not a client because I'm not a hooker. Repeat—I AM NOT A HOOKER!"

I felt a tap on my shoulder.

"You know, you could be," said an eleven-foot-tall man wearing a purple velvet blazer and high-heeled boots. "With the right management, I mean."

"Fuck off!"

"Here's my card," he said. "My office hours are ten p.m.to five a.m., with extended hours on Fridays and Saturdays."

"My daughter's way out of your league, asshole!" my mother yelled from the speaker.

"Sara?" the man said, addressing my phone. "Is that you?"

Oh my God.

"She doesn't need a common street manager, so piss off!" Mom yelled.

"Holy crap, Sara, she looks just like you! With lighter hair."

"I said piss off, Jefferson!"

"You're Jiggly Jeff?" I said, recalling the name from a few years back. He was Mom's bodyguard for about six months, but she fired his sorry ass when she heard he was working the street. "I pictured you way heavier."

"Keto diet," he said. "You should try it. Help you get rid of that extra fifteen pounds."

"My daughter's beautiful the way she is, you miserable mother fu—"

I hit the "end call" button, even though as a rule I never cut my mother off when she was calling a street pimp a miserable motherfucker. I'd make a point of apologizing profusely later. Right now I just needed to go somewhere and kill myself.

I returned to Ian's car. As soon as I slid into the passenger seat, I closed the window and pressed the recline button until I was flat on my back and no longer visible to anyone outside.

After a few moments of silence, Ian dared to speak. "Five thousand a night?"

"You have a problem with that, billionaire?" I said, instantly defensive.

"No," he said. "It's just that you told me your mother was a trophy wife."

"She was," I said. "Once. But after her last divorce she realized that she could make just as much running her own business as she could marrying and divorcing yet another asshole, so she became an independent contractor. And if you don't like the way she earns her money, that's your problem, not mine. I support and respect my mother's choices so don't even *think* of criticizing her in my presence."

"I wasn't going to criticize her," he said. "I'm just saying, if you support and respect hookers, why did you flip out when I thought you were one? And why are you so upset about the picture of us?"

"Because 'hooking' is open-air human trafficking. The women do all the work and then the pimps give them their 'cut,' which amounts to slave wages. My mother forged her own career path. She chooses her own clients, she sets her own hours, and she demands her clients pay her the kind of money she deserves. And if there's a bodyguard involved, she signs *his* paycheck, not the other way around."

He grew quiet for a moment. "Listen, I'm sorry I didn't tell you my real name," he finally said. "But you have to understand—"

"I don't have to understand anything, billionaire," I interrupted, not interested in anything he had to say. "You're a liar and a phony and I don't owe you shit. Can you just please call your team of three-thousand-dollar-an-hour lawyers and make this go away?"

"Can you please stop calling me 'billionaire' like it's my legal first name?"

"Sorry," I said. "Can you call your lawyers and make this go away, *Sir* Billionaire?"

He let out an annoyed sigh. "To answer your question, no, the lawyers can't make this go away. You have to pay off the photographers before they publish the pictures. Once the cat's out of the bag, you're screwed."

"So you've been in this position before?" I said.

"No," he said, not looking me in the eye. "Not me. I make a point of not doing stupid stuff like paying for sex. But my father goes through this about five times a year. He practically has the words 'extortion expense' as a line item on his profit and loss statement."

I closed my eyes. Up until this moment, I'd marked tomorrow on my calendar as "worst day of my life." But evidently today was going to claim the title instead. "No one's questioning it," I said. "Everyone took one look at the headlines and believed what they read. My friends. My family. My thesis advisor. My ex. And those were just the texts I've read so far."

My phone pinged again.

"No one's questioning it on my end, either," Ian said softly. "We're in this together, Clara."

I looked at him, disbelieving. And a little disgusted.

"Are you serious?" I said. "Do you really believe that?"

"Yes."

"You really think you and I are in the same boat?"

"Yes," he repeated, getting a little defensive. "You're not the only one whose picture is all over the internet. I'm right there beside you. The difference is, they didn't publish your name."

"Right. Lucky me. I'm just 'two-dollar whore.'"

"And I'm the sonofabitch who hired you. Prostitutes get forgiven. The men who hire them are branded pure evil for life."

I wasn't interested in his bullshit rationalization. Yeah, people in general had a better opinion of hookers than they did of johns. But Ian wasn't a person in general. He was some spoiled, lying rich fuck named Ian Dunning. "Don't even try to kid yourself that we're in the same boat," I said. "We're not even on the same planet. You have enough money to pay God to turn back time so that none of this ever happened to you. You want to know how much I make as a PhD candidate?"

"Less than me, but—"

"Thirty-six thousand dollars a year, Ian. In New York City. I can't even afford a subscription to the newspapers and gossip columns that are destroying my reputation, much less afford a lawyer to sue them for slander."

"I'm not going to abandon you. I promise, Clara. You want to sue these bastards?" he said, gesturing to the phone in my hand. "Say the word, I'll take care of the legal fees."

Yeah, sure he would. My mind traveled back to how happy I'd been just fifteen minutes earlier. I'd been standing in line at a coffee shop, wishing I'd let Ian speak his mind and trying to think up an excuse to go running back, when I suddenly realized that my keys were still stuck in his ignition. And there it was like a godsend—my excuse. I'd plowed through the crowded coffee shop and then bolted back down 63rd Street, happier than I'd been in years.

But that was fifteen minutes ago. Everything had changed. Ian and I were no longer two simple people on the verge of falling in love. Now Ian was a lying prick billionaire and I was an underpaid whore. We didn't even know each other. And we had nothing in common. I couldn't bear to even look him in the eye.

"You didn't even tell me your real name," I said. "Why should I believe anything you say?"

CHAPTER 24

IAN

She didn't trust me. And I didn't blame her. If I were her, I wouldn't trust me, either. But less than a half hour ago, we had been on the verge of something real. I had to find a way to get back to that place again. I had to make her trust me again. But based on the song she was currently singing, it wasn't going to be easy.

I listened as she lay on her back, moving her pointer fingers side to side in a sing-song motion.

Iaann Dundunfordsomer Jingleheimerschmidt
His name is my name, too.

"I said I was sorry," I said.

"And yet ten years of higher education is still flushed down the toilet, isn't it?" she said. "Along with my reputation, my life's work, and all hope for the future." She began tapping her foot.

Whenever we go out, the people always shout—

"Just tell me what you want me to do," I said.

"Trust me when I tell you that you don't want an honest answer to that question," she said.

There goes Ian Dun dadun dundundun—

The sarcasm was starting to get on my nerves. "Could you please stop singing for a second, Clara, and just let me—"

"Please, call me Ms. Zapatadadadingdong," she said. "It's Norwegian for 'someone just fucking kill me already.'"

"May I please finish a sentence?"

"Why, so you can lie some more?"

"No, so I can explain."

"Fine, billionaire," she said. "Go ahead. Explain."

"First of all, I'm not a billionaire, okay? My father is. I'm just his heir apparent. And that makes me a perfect target for gold diggers, blackmailers, and paparazzi. A lot of people out there know me on sight. But you didn't. I didn't tell you my real name because—"

I cut myself off mid-sentence. There was suddenly a far more urgent problem at hand. An unmarked white van was pulling into a parking spot on the opposite side of the street about fifty yards ahead of us. I immediately recognized the driver.

I quickly reclined my seat.

"Thank you for lowering yourself to my level," Clara said. "But I'm leaving, so don't waste your time."

She started to sit up, but instinctively, I flung my right arm over her torso. "Stay down."

"What the hell?" she said, attempting to push away my arm.

"Just stay down," I repeated. "My side windows are tinted but the windshield isn't. If you sit up, he'll be able to see you."

"Who'll be able to see me?"

Still holding her down, I clumsily picked up my phone with my left hand. Raising it above the dashboard, I snapped a few blind pictures.

"This is bullshit," she said, grabbing the door handle. "I'm leaving."

I pressed down harder, this time grabbing her elbow tight. "I'm sorry, Clara. But I can't let you leave."

"Are you threatening me?" she said, grabbing my arm with both hands and struggling in vain to break free of my grip.

"There's a threat to you," I said. "But I'm not it. And once you step out of this car, there's nothing I or anyone else on earth can do to help you."

She dug her nails into my skin. "I said let go of me!"

I didn't care if she drew blood. Once she stepped out of the car, it was all over for her. I couldn't let that happen.

"Look," I said, holding up my camera so she could see the picture I'd just taken. "Do you see that white van?"

She looked at the photo. "What about it?"

"There's a guy inside named Tom Carter. He's one of the most notoriously persistent paparazzi on earth, and the minute either of us gets out of this car, we're both back in the headlines."

She removed her fingernails from my flesh. "You're saying we have a stalker?"

"I'm saying *I* have a stalker," I clarified. "You just happen to be in the wrong place at the wrong time."

She let go of my arm. "It's amazing how much better this day keeps not getting."

I let go of her elbow but kept my arm protectively across her waist. "I know I haven't earned your trust, but I'm just going to ask you to believe me on this one. Everything will be okay if you just stay on your back and don't move."

"That's what all my clients say."

"Can you just promise to stay down? Please?"

"I promise to stay down," she said. "It appears I don't really have a choice in the matter, do I?"

At last, I removed my arm. "I have a restraining order against him," I explained as I massaged my fresh flesh wounds. "If he comes within one hundred feet of me, he goes to jail. Which means he can't climb onto the hood of my car and take a picture. But if either of us sits up straight or gets out, he can legally take as many pictures of us as he wants with his long-range camera and there's not a damn thing we can do about it."

"You can't just call your daddy and have the guy killed?"

"You know what?" I said, beginning to lose my patience. "The sarcasm really isn't helping me find us a way out of this. So do you think you could lose the attitude for five freaking seconds? Do you think you could do that for me, Clara?"

CHAPTER 25

CLARA

I think I could not. My mother had once observed that if MTV ever decided to reboot *Jersey Shore*, I could be cast as Clara "The Attitude" Zapata. And believe me, once someone flipped on the Zapatatude switch, it was pretty hard to turn it back off again.

"*You're* going to figure out a way to get us out of this?" I said.

"Yes."

"You?"

"Yes."

"The man who couldn't figure out a way to get into his own house."

"That was a fluke."

"Or his own car."

"I admit that intellectually this hasn't been the proudest day of my life," he said, his tone pissier by the minute. "But need I remind you that I didn't exactly get what you'd call a good night's sleep last night? But in spite of all that, I'm trying to do you a favor—"

"Do me a favor and don't do me any favors," I snapped. "You've already made today the worst day of my life, which is no small accomplishment considering what tomorrow was supposed to be."

"Do you think I'm enjoying this?" he said. "Because I'd rather spend a week trapped in a prison cell with a hyena than spend another minute in this car with you!"

"And I'd rather spend a week trapped in an elevator with a fart than spend another minute with you!"

"You know what?" he said. "Go ahead. Do it. Sit up and show Carter your face. Or better yet, just leave. I'm trying to protect you from getting your picture splattered all over the internet a thousand more times, but if existing in the same space as me is so goddamned tortuous, you're welcome to go on your merry way."

"What does it matter how many more pictures hit cyberspace? The whole world already knows I'm a two-dollar whore. How could a few more pictures on PerezHilton.com make it any worse than it already is?"

Grabbing his phone, he scrolled through his texts and clicked on a link. "Here," he said. "Look at the picture."

I looked. "Why are you showing me a picture of a naked woman?"

He grabbed back the phone and clicked another link.

"I meant this one," he said, showing me the picture of him paying me two bucks for my services.

I turned away. "Thanks, I've seen it."

"Just look at it," he said. "Please."

I reluctantly complied, taking the phone and looking at myself in all my whorish glory. "Wow. In retrospect, I should have worn my pink lipstick. It goes much better with my left nipple."

He pried the phone back out of my hand, his eyes assiduously scanning the picture for my nipple like it was Waldo. "Where?"

"On my left boob," I said. "Same place it always is."

He looked at my boob in the photo. "A little bit of exposed bra," he said, handing the phone back. "Nobody will notice. And anyway, I'm not talking about your boob. I'm talking about your face."

I looked at my hideous lipstick-smeared visage. "What about it?"

"You're barely recognizable," he said. "The picture's taken in profile, half your face is hidden by your hair, and the part that you can see is smeared with lipstick. No one will recognize you."

"I've gotten about ten texts so far asking me what made me stoop to this level. People recognize me."

"Who are the texts from?" he said.

"My mother. My thesis advisor. My friends."

"Exactly," he said. "People who could spot you in a crowd of a thousand faces. But if you walk down this street right now, no one's going to associate you with the woman in the picture. Your face is different. Your hair is different. Your clothes are different. It's like you and the woman in the picture aren't even related."

"Then why can't I get out of the car?" I asked.

"Because the minute Carter sees you step out of my car, he's taking your picture. And he'll compare that picture to the picture from this morning and figure out it's one and the same person. And from there it's only a matter of time before he plasters every detail of your life across the internet. If you want to keep your name out of the tabloids, you're going to have to lay low for a while. Literally."

"So I just have to lie here on my back until this sonofabitch gets tired and—oh my God, no matter what I say, I sound like a hooker. I should just go buy a peekaboo bra and a pair of crotchless panties and get it over with already."

I waited for him to reply. He did not.

"Stop looking at me like that," I said.

"Like what?"

"I'm wearing a pair of fully-crotched briefs that I bought on clearance at Walmart. We're talking about the photographer."

"Right," he said. "Carter. Don't expect him to get tired anytime soon. Like I said, he's extremely persistent. We could be waiting another ten hours."

My one-track mind immediately went to its favorite subject. "What if he has to pee?"

"He'll do it in the street."

"Gross!"

"He can make a hundred thousand dollars off the right picture or video footage," Ian said. "He'll do whatever it takes."

"So we just have to stay like this for the next ten hours?"

"Of course not," he said. "I told you, I'll come up with a plan. Just give me a few minutes to think."

While Ian was lying on his back "thinking" (which I was beginning to suspect was a bold word for what was going on in that head of his), I was lying on my back doing some thinking of my own.

"What if *I* have to pee?" I said. "*I'm* not doing it in the street. Not even for a hundred thousand dollars."

"I think there's an empty water bottle in the back seat."

Ah. The "plan" was already taking shape. "Can you take another picture of the guy? I'd like to see the face of the man who may or may not snap a picture of me taking a wee in the back of your car."

Ian raised his arm above the dashboard and snapped a few more blind pictures, then handed me the phone.

I looked. Carter was half hidden behind his van, a long-range camera in his hand. "Holy crap, is that Army camo he's wearing?"

"I said he was persistent. Not intelligent."

I expanded the picture with my thumb and forefinger so I could get a better look at my new personal photographer. God, what a weasel. Seriously. He looked like an actual weasel. Long skinny body with a tiny head, ratty brown hair, and huge ears. All that was missing was the monkey chasing him all around the mulberry bush. And God, that freaking camo.

"How stupid can a person be?" I said. "Should we text him and tell him he's not exactly blending in with the two white vehicles he's standing between?"

Suddenly I noticed something. The white car parked behind Carter's van was a Hyundai Santa Fe. I expanded the photo to maximum size. Sure enough, there was a tiny dent on the front left bumper.

"You've got to be kidding me," I mumbled.

"What?" Ian said.

I tossed Ian's phone to the side and picked up my own.

It only rang once before Mom answered.

"Is your Santa Fe parked on 63rd Street?" I said before she even had a chance to say hello.

"Yes," she said.

"Holy shit, Mom, seriously? You're at the bar again?"

"No," Mom said. "I'm at the bar still."

"Since ten last night?"

"Yes," she said. "Paulie caught his dick boyfriend cheating on him again. We were up talking until four in the morning, so I just slept in the office. And how do you know where my car is?"

"I was so drunk last night that I accidently fell asleep in Ian's car. And then this morning he accidentally locked his keys and phone inside so I drove him to his house so he could pick up his spare. We just got back. We're parked about ten doors down from Paulie's."

"And are you still with Ian?"

"Yeah," I said. "And we're in some serious shit here. There's a photographer hiding between your car and his van. As soon as I sit upright or get out of the car, I'm going to be back in the tabloids again."

"Don't worry," Mom said. "This is Mommy's area of expertise. Just give me a sec, I'll think of something."

"I'm going to get her out of this, Ms. Zapata!" Ian said loudly enough for her to hear. "I just need an hour or so to come up with a plan!"

"Okay, I have a plan," Mom said.

"Already?" Ian said.

"Is your car nearby?" Mom asked me.

"It's right behind Ian's."

"And what about my Santa Fe?" she said. "Is it behind the van or in front of it?"

"Behind it."

"Perfect," Mom said. "Here's what we're going to do. I'll send Paulie out to pick up my car. He'll drive it around to the alley behind the bar. Then I'll walk up 63rd

Street and distract the photographer. Paulie will keep watch from the window, and when he sees I've got the photographer's full attention, he'll ring you. That will be your signal to run inside the bar. Paulie will leave my car keys on the counter and you leave your keys for me. Then you and Ian go out the back exit and make your escape in the Santa Fe. I'll take your car for the next few days. You two lay low until all this blows over."

"Thanks, Mom," I said. "You're a lifesaver."

"Just keep me in the loop so I know you're safe. And turn off the tracker on your phone."

"I will."

"Paulie's on his way out right now. Be ready to run in five minutes."

CHAPTER 26

IAN

Wow. Just. Wow.

While I was lying there thinking of a way to bore a hole through the floor of my Toyota so we could slither like snakes under parked cars until we were out of Carter's line of sight, Clara's mom had given clear-cut instructions for what promised to be a perfectly executed escape. And it had taken her all of about one second to come up with it.

"I'm officially impressed," I said.

"With what?" Clara said.

"Your mom. She's really cool. Like way, way cooler than my dad. He would have just sent somebody here to break Carter's legs and smash his camera."

"She has a lot of high-profile clients," Clara explained. "She knows how to evade unwanted attention."

Her phone pinged, and a text bubble popped up.

"It's time," she said.

Cautiously, we both lifted our heads and looked out the dashboard window. There was now a black Lexus where the Santa Fe had been. A woman in dark glasses and a crimson dress was lying on her back across its hood in an extremely sexy pose. Sara. Her plan was working like a charm. Carter was facing the opposite direction, very eagerly engaged in his impromptu photo shoot.

"She's got his full attention," Clara said. "Let's go."

We quickly grabbed our things and snuck out of the car. Hunched over, we ran to Clara's car and grabbed her duffle bag out of the back seat. Careful to remain hidden from any prying eyes, we sprinted up the block and through the front door of Paulie's. A tall man with dark hair, presumably Paulie, was waiting for us.

"You've got to move quick," he said.

"I owe you one, Paulie," Clara said as she handed him her car keys.

"Don't worry about it," he said. "Just hurry up and get out of here. I don't know how much longer your mom can keep the photographer distracted."

"This way," Clara said to me, gesturing toward a door that said 'Employees Only.' We passed through an office and headed toward the neon exit sign. A moment later, Clara was cautiously peeking her head out into the back alley.

"Are we alone?" I whispered.

"No one's there," she whispered. "Come on, let's go."

A minute later, we were pulling onto Park Avenue in Clara's mom's Santa Fe. Free at last.

Or so we thought. Over the course of the next fifteen minutes, we only managed to get from the corner of Park and 63rd to the corner of Park and 64th. As we crawled forward at a snail's pace, my heart began to pound. Clara was one inch away from being dragged into the darkest depths of tabloid hell. I'd been there a million times before and I could handle it. But Clara couldn't. And shouldn't have to. She was an innocent victim. Yeah, she had passed out in my car and technically started it all. Whatever. One dumb mistake shouldn't mean she was branded a two-dollar whore for the rest of her life.

I reached over to her side of the car and honked the horn, long and loud.

"That's not going to work," she said. "We're sandwiched in like sardines."

"We have to get out of town," I said, sure she could hear the desperation in my voice. "Fast."

"Why?" she said, naïvely calm. "We're safe now."

"We've barely moved," I said, scrutinizing the cars behind us in the mirror. "Carter's still only one block away."

"Exactly," she said. "He's still standing behind his van thinking *we're* still hiding in your Toyota. You said it yourself, he could be waiting there for the next ten hours."

"He's not exactly the only guy in town with a camera. Guys like him are vultures. They travel in packs."

"Maybe so," she said. "But no one else knows where to find us."

"I would be extremely surprised if that was true," I said. "Have you asked yourself how Carter found us?"

"I just assumed he was the one who took the picture this morning and was returning to the scene of the crime."

"The picture from this morning's a grainy piece of crap. Carter's a pro, with the best camera money can buy. No way did he take that picture."

"Then how'd he know where to find us?"

"The same way everyone else will know where to find us. He saw the name of a restaurant or store in the background, looked up the address online, and then made a beeline to 63rd Street. And if he could find us with the click of a mouse—"

She gasped, and it was clear that she was beginning to realize the true gravity of our situation.

"If he could find us," she said, "so can anyone else."

CHAPTER 27

CLARA

"Exactly," Ian said.

Fuck me. Just when I thought the worst was over. "So you think there could be others on the way?"

"I don't think it," he said. "I know it."

"But won't they get held up by the traffic?"

"Not if they walk or bus or parachute in," he said. "Carter works for a network. That's why he arrived in the unmarked van. But amateurs can do just as much damage as a professional. More, even. I don't have a restraining order against anyone but Carter. Which means anyone with a camera phone can climb up on the hood of the car and start taking pictures."

"Isn't that illegal?" I said. "Trespassing on private property or intimidation or something?"

"You think they care about that?" he said.

"Shit." I had never realized how lucky I was to have a starring role on *Lifestyles of the Broke and Obscure*. I'd only been the subject of tabloid scrutiny for one hour and already my life was in shambles. How did celebrities stand it? And how much worse must it be for someone like Ian? Movie stars and politicians actively sought public attention. Ian's apparent celebrity status was uninvited and unwanted. It was becoming clearer to me why he lived in isolation at the end of a mile-long driveway, worked alone from home, and had tinted windows on his car. He wasn't a hermit because he wanted to be. He was a hermit because he had to be.

"When did your first text come in?" he asked, interrupting my thoughts.

"Less than an hour ago, I think."

"Yeah, mine, too," he said. "So that means that the picture probably hit the internet two hours ago at most. Which means it's just about time for the swarm to make landfall."

He was trying to maintain a calm demeanor. But if we were playing poker right now, I'd be wiping the floor with him. He was breathing in visibly deep breaths. There were beads of sweat on his forehead. And his paranoid eyes were glued to the side mirror, desperately searching for oncoming paparazzi.

He was in panic mode, and it was contagious. I wasn't as quick on my feet as my street-savvy mother, but I did know that my only hope of getting out of this mess with my life intact was to stay hidden from the cameras.

So I did what I always did in a crisis: channeled Mom.

"If I can get to the right lane, I can turn onto 66th," I said, tensely gripping the wheel. "From there it'll just be a matter of getting to I-87."

I realized that what I was suggesting was easier said than done. The traffic was more than bumper-to-bumper. It was door-to-door. Park Avenue looked like a goddamned impound lot. I was no more in control of the situation than Ian was.

"Everything's going to be fine," Ian said even though his nervous tone indicated he didn't believe a word of what he was saying. "We just need to remain calm and not do anything to draw attention to ourselves. There!" he cried out, pointing.

"What?"

"An opening!" he said with the enthusiasm of a little boy who had just spotted a roadside carnival. "In front of the red car to the right!"

Ahead of us was a little red Porsche with an enormous black dog in its sliver of a back seat. There was about a half a car length of space between it and the car in front of it. It was just enough room for me to nose the Santa Fe into.

But there was one very, very big problem.

"I can't do it," I said.

"Just veer to the right!" Ian said. "Get as close as you can without hitting him. He'll take the hint!"

"It's not the car I'm afraid of hitting. It's the dog. Look at him. He's got his neck three feet out the window. If I get in too close, I'll lop his head off."

"Who the hell puts a dog that size into a Porsche anyway?" Ian grumbled as he rolled down his window.

"Ian, don't—"

But it was too late. Ian's upper body was sticking out the window.

"Hey, asshole!" he yelled to the Porsche's driver. "Do you think you can tell your giraffe to pull his head in the car? People are trying to move here!"

"Hey, shit for brains," the man in the Porsche yelled back, "do you think you can suck my cock for lunch?"

"Ever hear of animal cruelty, dickface! He's going to get crushed to death back there!"

"I didn't design the car, motherfucker! It's not my fault the backseat's so tight!"

"Maybe you should have thought of that before you went to the pet shelter and adopted a buffalo, fucktard!"

I pulled Ian back into the car before he and his new friend had a chance to exchange any more Manhattanesque terms of endearment. "Way to not attract attention."

"I can get past this asshole," Ian said, pointing to the steering wheel. "Let me drive."

"A Chinese fire drill?" I said. "Here? There isn't even enough space to open the car doors."

"Climb over the console," he said as he unbuckled his seatbelt. "We'll swap seats."

"Absolutely not," I said. "You're not behaving rationally and I'm not going to let you get into a wreck with my mother's car."

"We have to move and we have to move fast. If I get into a wreck, I'll buy your mom a Maserati."

Right. Billionaire. I kept forgetting.

"Okay," I reluctantly agreed, "but you have to promise to drive safely."

"I promise to drive safely."

Against my better judgement, I put the car into park and began climbing over the console to the passenger seat. At the same time, Ian began climbing to the driver's seat. It was a tight squeeze and an extremely awkward transition, to put it mildly.

"Maybe in retrospect this wasn't a great plan," Ian said as we inadvertently rubbed our asses together.

"You think?" I said as I put my foot on his ass cheek and gave it a kick-push.

"Ow!" he said.

"Just be glad I changed out of my heels," I said when I finally made it to the passenger seat.

I looked over at Ian. He was smushed into the driver's seat, his knees pressed against the dashboard, his chest about one inch from the steering wheel. His left hand was manically feeling up the door panel. "Where the hell's the seat adjuster in this thing?"

"Isn't it under the seat?" I said, trying not to laugh.

"Who the hell puts the adjuster under the seat?"

"Mercury does," I said. "In my car, there's a bar under the seat."

"Do you know where the adjuster is for cars manufactured this century?"

"No," I said. "My mom always drives. I've never had to adjust her seat. Gas!"

"What?"

"Hit the gas, we're moving!" I said.

He hit the gas and started inching toward the Porsche.

"We're going to make it!" Ian cried, exuberant. "I'm going to get past the Porsche and we're going to make it out of the city!"

It was extremely difficult to keep a straight face. He was quite the sight, with his knees and chest pressed against the steering wheel proclaiming "we're going to make it!" with the joy of an escaped Allied prisoner spotting the French border on the horizon.

"Stop laughing at me!" he yelled.

"I'm not laughing!" I said. Or would have said if I wasn't laughing so hard. I kept picturing him on a firetruck carnival ride, going round and round in circles in a tiny red engine and pulling the string that made the bell go ding-ding.

"Do I really look that stupid?" he said as he inched past the Porsche and sidled into the right lane.

I wiped my eyes. "Yes."

"We made it," he said, turning right. "Now do you think you can help me out here?"

"Did you try the side of the seat?"

"Yes," he said. "I keep pushing a button but the seat isn't moving."

"Try the bottom of the seat," I said.

"I did," he said. "There's some kind of handle but it won't budge."

Still plastered to the steering wheel, he pulled onto Third Avenue, where the speed of traffic increased to about thirty miles an hour.

"I can't keep driving like this at this speed," he said. "I'm going to get us both killed."

"There's no place to pull over."

"Just figure something out! You're the doctoral candidate!"

"Not in physics, I'm not."

"This isn't physics! It's up and down and forward and back."

"Exactly," I said. "Physics."

"Just find the damn adjuster, Clara!"

As entertaining as his current posture was, I had to agree that it was both unsafe and untenable. I unbuckled my seatbelt. "Just hold still and promise not to enjoy this too much."

I scooted my behind over to the left, turned my body ninety degrees, and inserted my right arm into the tight space between the steering wheel and Ian's lap. As my hand felt around for the adjuster, it became enormously clear to me that my previous supposition that nothing could be more awkwardly personal than our recent ass-to-ass encounter was misguided.

"Oh my God," I said. "What did I *just* say about not enjoying this too much?"

"I'm sorry," he said. "It's nature at work. I have no control over it. And your gigantic boob rubbing against my arm isn't exactly helping!"

"For the love of God, man," I said as my hand searched for the adjuster, "it's only been five seconds!"

"Actually, it's been eight months," he said. "Nature's been ready to make a big comeback for a while now."

God, where the hell did Mom hide the seat adjuster? "Could you kindly tell nature to take it down a notch?"

"No," Ian said. "He hasn't seen the light of day for eight months. I can't help it if he's reaching for the stars."

"At least yours is a he," I mumbled. "Tyler nicknamed his Irma."

While the crease of my elbow made bestest buddies with nature, my fingers ran back and forth along the bottom of the seat until they at last found a knob.

"I think I found it!"

"Thank God," Ian said.

I pushed the knob backwards and down, and Ian's upper body started to unglue itself from the steering wheel.

"Tell me when it's good," I said.

He sighed deeply. "It's good."

"I meant the seat!"

"That's good, too," he said, taking another deep breath as he rolled his shoulders. "Oh my God, I'm so happy."

I sat back up and re-buckled myself in.

"Thank you," Ian said with a relieved sigh as he rubbed his neck. "You have no idea how good it feels—"

"I know how good it feels," I said. "This isn't exactly my first rodeo."

"I was talking about the car seat."

"Oh. Right."

We spent the next ten minutes driving in silence. It was an odd ten minutes. By this point, we'd given each other a mutual ass massage, made boob-to-arm contact, and been co-conspirators in an erection. And yet, surprisingly, there was no awkwardness between us. Thinking it over, I supposed it made perfect sense. Imagine how much more pleasant lockdown would have been if everyone had greeted their colleagues and debate opponents by rubbing asses instead of elbows. Throw in a neighborly boob rub and a friendly erection, and we would have achieved world peace by now.

At any rate, at this point in our increasingly personal relationship, no topic of conversation seemed off the table. And there was something I was really, really curious about.

"So," I said. "Eight months, huh?"

CHAPTER 28

IAN

Normally I would not openly discuss this with someone I'd only known for seven hours, but since Clara's elbow and my dick had already shared what you might call a moment, I felt strangely comfortable talking about my eight-month-long dry spell.

"I haven't had sex with anyone since Greta. If what we did deserved to be called sex, that is."

"That bad?" she said.

"Depends on whose point of view you're talking about," I said. "For me, it was mad, passionate lovemaking. For her, it was a monthly reminder that the heating bill was due."

She was trying to hide a smile.

"Go ahead, laugh all you want," I said. "But I'd like to hear how well you and Irma got along."

"Holy crap," she said. "Did I say that out loud?"

"You did."

She shrugged. "Let's just say that she lived up to her name. Although Mabel or Ethel might have been a better choice."

Now it was my turn to laugh. "That bad?"

"It wasn't bad when it actually happened," she said. "It's just that it hadn't happened in six months."

I wasn't sure I'd heard her right. "How could it have been six months if you just broke up two weeks ago?"

"The abstinence was Tyler's idea," she said. "We were revirgining."

"You were *what?*"

"Abstaining from sex for six months to reclaim our virginity before the wedding night." She seemed to be thinking it over. "At least, supposedly that was the purpose. In retrospect, I think he just didn't want to have sex with me."

As my present anatomical state would indicate, it was kind of hard for me to believe that any man with a beating heart would willingly abstain from sex with a ready and waiting Clara Zapata. I wondered if Tyler was one of those macho assholes who only enjoyed sex when it felt like a conquest, like it was 1958 and he was getting a girl to surrender her virtue.

But enough about Tyler. I was much more interested in Clara's perspective on the matter.

"So what did you do for . . ." I paused, searching my mind for the right word. "Fulfillment?"

"Isn't it obvious?" she said. "Look at me."

I looked at her. I liked what I saw. But I had no idea what I was supposed to be seeing. "I think I'm missing something."

"I ate," she said. "A lot."

I glanced over again. I supposed she was what overcritical people might politely call "curvy." But I, for one, was a big fan of curves, particularly in comparison to the living, breathing female skeletons I'd spent my multimillion-dollar life around. Despite a breathtaking amount of medical evidence refuting their benefits, visible ribcages were still all the rage among the weekends-in-the-Hamptons crowd.

"Is it alright if I get a little personal here?" I said.

"More personal than you are right now?" she said, glancing down at nature, which was still very much at work.

"Not quite as personal as that," I said. "But still pretty personal. To women, at least."

"I see," she said. "All right then. I'm on a thirty-day cycle, the cramps are pretty bad, and my favorite brand is Tampax."

"Thanks for the info, but it's actually more personal than that."

"Wow," she said. "He wants details. Okay, here goes. Slender on days one and five, super-absorbent days two through four."

"Good God, woman, not that personal!"

She pretended to puzzle over what could possibly be on my mind. "I was nineteen and he was twenty-one?"

"How about you just let me ask my question?"

"Sorry," she said. "Go ahead."

I took a moment to steel my nerves, then decided to just spit it out. "How much do you weigh?"

I got the response I expected. A heaping pile of silence served with a smattering of death stare.

"Why?" she said. "Do you think I'm overweight?"

"We're not talking about me. We're talking about you. Do *you* think you're overweight?"

"I'm certainly not skinny."

"What's so great about skinny?" I said.

"I don't know," she said. "Ask the entire world. They seem to think very highly of it."

"Last time I checked, the entire world is a complete moron. Don't you read internet news?"

"I don't need to read internet news to know that I'm above average weight for someone my size. All I have to do is look in the mirror."

"How tall are you?"

"Five six."

"And what's considered to be the medically healthy weight for a woman your height?"

"According to the Mayo Clinic, between one hundred twenty-three and one hundred thirty-seven pounds."

It didn't surprise me that she knew the Mayo Clinic's clinical answer off the top of her head. "And how much do you weigh?" I asked, reiterating my original question.

"Can we just talk about my period some more? I prefer Motrin for cramps but Aleve will do in a pinch."

"Thanks for sharing, but I think I already know all I need to know about you on the menstrual front. What I want is for you to tell me how much you weigh. I want to hear you say the number out loud."

"Why?"

"So I can tell you how nuts you are."

"You don't think asking a woman her weight is a little bit personal?"

"*You're* telling *me* about personal?" I said. "I'm currently breaking the record for the world's longest public hard-on here. I'm pretty sure you owe me one."

"I'm pretty sure I already gave you one."

"Very funny," I said. "Did anyone ever tell you you're a wiseass?"

"Yes."

"How much do you weigh!"

She scrunched her face like a stubborn kid whose mommy was forcing her to say she was sorry. "How much do *you* weigh?"

As if any man who wasn't a professional wrestler was embarrassed to admit his weight. "One hundred eighty-seven pounds. Five foot eleven and three quarters, starting to gray at the temples, and eighteen years old with another freshman from my dorm. And last but not least," I said, pointing to my groin area, "this is how I spent the entirety of tenth grade geometry class because Mr. Foley just *had* to seat me behind Elena Rodriguez. So there, I win. Let's see you out-personal that."

She knew she'd been beat. You can always count on a good old-fashioned open-air erection story to outdo everyone else in the conversation circle. You should hear me at Christmas dinner. I'm the goddamned life of the party.

"Fine," she said. "I'm a hundred and thirty-seven pounds. Top of my weight class. Feel free to congratulate me."

"Congratulations," I said. "I happen to think you have a very nice body."

"In a fetish magazine sort of way."

"For the last time, you're not overweight!" I said. "Or hefty or pudgy or pleasingly plump!"

"How about *on the heavy side?*"

"If by 'on the heavy side' you mean that you have a sweet cuddle body, then yeah," I said, "you're on the heavy side."

"Oh my God!" she said. "Did you just say I'm on the heavy side?"

What was it that Freud said again? Wait, now I remembered—*Give up, Ian, you're never going to win this one.* But I refused to back down. I'd seen too many of my father's wives and lady friends obsess over their weight, only to look about ten times worse once they'd starved their way into skeletal versions of their former selves. Clara was beautiful the way she was, and if any sexist pig thought otherwise, that was his problem, not hers. "If your healthy weight is between one-twenty-three and one-thirty-seven, then one-thirty is the median, right?"

"Right."

"So that means you are, in fact, seven points in favor of the heavy side. Which, in my personal opinion, is not and should not be a problem."

"Tell Tyler that," she said, turning away with a huff.

I felt instantly guilty. For a minute there, I'd forgotten that tomorrow was supposed to be her wedding day, and that the reason it wasn't was the fifteen pounds that were the topic of our current discussion. But to be fair, she made it easy to forget she had a freshly broken heart. If she hadn't told me about her breakup, I never would have guessed. She didn't act like someone who'd just been unceremoniously dumped. When Greta fired me, I was a total basket case for months, and anyone standing within a mile of me could see it.

But just because Clara didn't display her broken heart didn't mean she didn't have one. There was no question that she had a lot of depth and character. And such people have very deep feelings, whether they let the world see it or not. I suspected she had been one of those kids raised to be tough, to have their cry and move on without burdening others with their feelings. Clara was hurting far more than she let on, perhaps more than she was willing to admit even to herself, much less to me.

"You know what?" I said. "Gladly."

"Gladly what?"

"Give me Tyler's number and I'll gladly call him right now and thank him for doing you the biggest favor of your life by buggering off for eternity."

Her expression softened. "It's sweet of you to say that, Ian. Really. But—"

"It's not sweet," I said. "It's the truth. You're not overweight. You're beautiful. And I'm sure you own a mirror, so I know you know it, too. But big or small, pretty or ugly, it shouldn't have mattered to Tyler. And frankly, I don't understand why it matters to you. You're getting your doctorate. You're going to be Dr. Zapata. I just don't understand why someone like you cares so much about her appearance."

She looked down, almost as if she were ashamed. "I care because I'm stupid."

"Bullshit," I said. "Tell that to Columbia University and Everglades National Park. You sure fooled them."

"I don't mean I'm stupid intellectually," she said. "I'm smart enough when it comes to book learning. I do good fieldwork and write incisive papers and all that. But when it comes to my personal life . . ." She trailed off.

"When it comes to your personal life . . .?" I prompted.

"It leaves a little to be desired."

"Like how?" I said.

"It's not bad, really," she said, thinking it over. "It's actually very good when it comes to family and friends.

And colleagues. And birds. It's just kind of a disaster area when it comes to men."

She didn't elaborate. But I really wanted to hear more. "So you've had other bad breakups?"

She stared out at the road ahead. "Three others in the last decade," she said quietly.

"Were they at least good while they lasted?"

"Yeah," she said. "They were great while they lasted. And I was very happy."

"So what went wrong?"

I saw her swallow. "I don't remember."

I wasn't going to let her off the hook that easily. "Yes, you do."

"You're right," she said. "I do."

I waited for her to elaborate. She did not.

"So?" I said.

"So what?"

"What went wrong?"

"They asked me to marry them."

It took me a moment to digest that one. "*Four* different guys have asked you to marry them?"

"Five if you count the drunken loser at the bar last night."

"Holy shit."

I couldn't help but notice that my voice sounded a little bit hostile. And the reason I sounded a little bit hostile was because I was more than a little bit jealous. I didn't like the idea of Clara being so popular with men. In fact, I was pretty sure I hated it. But nonetheless, I wanted to understand it.

"But if the relationships were so great and you were so happy, why did they end badly?"

She looked out the side window. "It was my fault," she mumbled.

"What was?"

"The unhappy endings," she said, this time a little more clearly. "They were my fault. All of them."

"I don't believe that."

"Believe it or don't. Your choice. But it's true."

"Can I ask what's so horribly wrong with you that you supposedly ruined every relationship you've ever been in?"

"You can ask," she said. "But you'll be sorry."

"I won't be sorry," I said. "Come on. Spill it."

CHAPTER 29

CLARA

Once upon a time, there was a little girl who believed in happily ever after. She lived in a four-thousand-square-foot castle whose shelves were filled with Disney DVDs and Hallmark movies and paperbacks whose covers were ninety percent chest. The little girl was a lover of all things beaked and feathered, her stepdaddy was a wealthy landowner, and her mother was Fabio's primary source of income.

One day, the little girl heard a strange rumbling sound coming from outside the castle, and she was so afraid she ran down the stairs to her mother's side.

"Mummy!" she cried as she looked out the front window. "What is that big van in the driveway? Has it come to take me away?"

"Heavens, no, my little one," said the girl's mother with a jolly laugh. "None shall ever take you from my loving arms. What you see before you is not a van, my sweet, but a moving truck."

"A moving truck?" said the little girl as she gazed upon the beastly machine. "What is this 'moving truck' of which you speak?"

"It's a sixteen-hundred-square-foot container that shall haul thy stepfather's shit to a land far, far away where he can live in peace and happiness with his new whore."

"But Mother," protested the little girl, "if Stepdaddy is departing never to return, why did he not tell me this morning when he departed for whatever the hell it is he does all day?"

"My sweet, naïve child," said the mother, "thy stepfather could not tell you he was leaving, for he does not yet know."

"But won't Stepdaddy be surprised when he returns and finds that all his worthless crap, including the ridiculous collection of antlers he didn't even hunt himself, has been spirited away by"—the little girl squinted, straining to read the words on the side of the truck—'Hunky College Movers?'"

"That he will," said the girl's mother. "But it shall be a mere trifling compared to the surprise Mommy's lawyers have in store for him."

At that moment, there came a loud pounding on the door. The girl looked out the window and was terrified at what she saw standing on the porch.

"Mother!" she cried. "Who is that extremely well-built twenty-year-old man knocking upon our door? And why does he not wear a shirt?"

"Do not fear, my darling," said the mother. "It is only Mover Evan, come to help Mommy with something in the bedroom. Wait here and play with your pretty toys, and Mommy shall return in forty minutes to an hour."

The mother unbuttoned the top button of her blouse and walked across the room to the front door.

"Mummy?" the girl said just as her mother grabbed the doorknob.

"Yes, my darling?"

"Will Mover Evan be my new stepdaddy?"

The mother laughed her jolly laugh. "Only if he owns the company, my dear."

My mom did a lot of things right, but she wasn't the world's greatest role model when it came to men. I couldn't say how many men had passed through her transom over the years (a transom is a window above a doorway, not a vagina, by the way), but Mom had given up on marriage—both real and trophy—by the time I was eleven.

I never met my real father, who had abandoned Mom while she was still very much in love with him and very much pregnant with me. Eight months pregnant, to be precise. As in she no longer had the fashion-model figure that was evidently the only reason my father had loved her in the first place. She was twenty-one and he was twenty-two, and they lived paycheck to paycheck and didn't own anything except towels. My father didn't want me in the first place, so there was nothing in the way of a custody battle. Mom's dreams were crushed and her heart was broken, but in terms of logistics, it was a relatively pain-free divorce.

Within the year, she got her girlish figure back, and along with it, a long line of men salivating outside her door. After a series of shallow relationships that lasted an average of six months and involved many expensive gifts that ended up at the pawn shop, she finally met the next man of her dreams. She was twenty-five, and I was four. Garret was older, sophisticated, and successful, and constantly told her what a beautiful treasure she was. Together they bought a four-bedroom house, complete with an in-ground pool and a set of matching BMWs in the driveway. Those first two years of marriage were the happiest of Mom's life. That is, until she told Garret she was ready to have another baby, at which time he told her that might be awkward, what with his twenty-year-old girlfriend due to give birth any day.

If Mom walked away from her second marriage every bit as brokenhearted as from her first, she at least walked away a little bit wiser and with far less financial worry. Along with the guarantee of a very healthy monthly alimony check, she walked off with the BMW and half the proceeds of the house sale.

And off she was to another series of relationships with men whose favorite thing to do was show her off at parties as "my girlfriend, Sara, a former lingerie model." She'd remind her boyfriends that she had a last name, and they'd remind her that they didn't give a shit. She'd then remind them that if they insisted on treating her like a trophy, she was okay with that, but jewelry and credit cards needed to be involved.

Yes, she was growing cynical. If men were going to treat her like a trophy, she was going to treat them like a bank account. But it wasn't all about the money. She was still only in her twenties, and many of her friends weren't even on their first marriages yet. Which meant that there was still hope of finding true and lasting love, complete with a white picket fence and a house full of children.

And then along came Aaron. He was sweet and funny and kind and made an average middle-class income. But Mom didn't care how much he did or didn't earn. She didn't marry him for his money, or lack thereof. She married him because he listened when she told him her stories. She married him because he introduced her to his friends as plain old Sara. But mostly, she married him because his favorite way to spend a Friday night was cuddling with her in front of the fireplace, and because her eight-year-old daughter called him "Daddy." Mom was sure he was the one, and he was. She was sure their marriage wouldn't end in divorce, and it didn't.

It ended with a car accident. She was twenty-nine and came out with a few bruises. He was thirty-two and died a month later. They had been married for eight months.

In addition to being devastated on the emotional front, she was panicked on the financial front. She'd given up her hefty alimony check from Garret in exchange for a lifetime of love with Aaron. Now both Aaron and Garret were gone. Aaron hadn't even had life insurance, and the medical bills from the accident ate up the bulk of her savings and pawn-shop earnings. She was left with less than five thousand dollars in joint savings and a house with barely enough equity to pay the realtor's sales commission. In short, she walked away from the funeral broke, both emotionally and financially.

She needed money and she needed it fast. But her only real work experience was modeling, and she'd aged out of the industry. She was already dipping into my education fund to pay for rent and food. In lieu of returning to work, she decided to return to what was historically her most reliable source of income: men. In her mind, she'd already found and lost the love of her life.

She'd never find another man who loved her like Aaron, so there was no point in trying. She put herself back on the wife market, content to offer herself up as marital eye-candy to a man content to be used for his money.

She found him. In spades. On her thirtieth birthday, less than a year after Aaron's death, she married Stephen. Stephen was egotistical, boorish, and thirty years older, but Mom didn't care. All that mattered was that he was a successful divorce lawyer who wanted a beautiful wife, and she was a beautiful woman who wanted a handsome income stream. Husband and wife played their parts beautifully. Mom clung to Stephen's arm at black-tie events and conspicuously bickered with the other trophy wives over whose husband was the most brilliant and successful and magnificent in the sack. In return, Stephen lavished her with jewelry, provided her with more credit cards than her designer wallet could hold, and bankrolled her education-addicted daughter's thirty-thousand-dollar-a-year private-school habit.

I was honestly pretty goddamned happy during the Stephen years. But Mom was not. She'd fallen out of love with husbands before, but Stephen was the first husband she hadn't loved in the first place. By their two-year anniversary, she had learned that living under the same roof with someone you can't stand and who can't stand you back was emotionally exhausting. She would have stuck it out if Stephen was just old, shallow, and boring. But when he wasn't playing the role of the world's most generous husband and stepfather, he was a spectacular bastard. Every day started and ended with a barrage of verbal and emotional abuse, and in between, he cheated on Mom with anything that had two legs and could breathe. It was when she found out that he was spending upwards of ten thousand dollars a month on high-class call girls that she decided she'd finally had enough. The way her lawyer argued it, it was a stated trophy marriage from the beginning, and while Mom had faithfully and assiduously fulfilled her end of the contract, Stephen had reneged on his. It was a reasonable argument, but there was one big problem: Stephen was a lawyer, too, and a damned good one. While the final divorce decree provided Mom with twenty thousand a month in alimony, it also stipulated that the payments would end upon Stephen's death. Stephen was already sixty years old, had a bad heart and about five thousand enemies. Mom could only rely on the alimony until Stephen had a heart attack or one of his former clients' ex-husbands shot him, and it was a miracle neither had happened already. She needed a backup plan.

She was still young and beautiful, so if she wanted a new rich husband, all she had to do was bat an eyelash. The problem was, she'd had enough. On the surface, trophy marriage looked like easy money. But the hidden price was being shackled to a prick. The charade never ended, and constantly pretending she loved a man she couldn't stand was unbearable. She decided she'd rather die than marry again.

The good news was, as Stephen's worst habit had so vividly illustrated, a woman didn't have to marry a man to make money off of him. There was a viable alternative that was every bit as lucrative as marriage, but offered a woman something a ring on her finger could not: freedom.

Mom's fourth marriage was her last, and her new, shackle-free career was up and running. She was thirty-two years old.

It was the night of the little girl's first formal dance. Only she wasn't a little girl anymore. She was sixteen years old and a junior in high school. Her old Disney DVDs were rotting in a landfill. The family bookshelf was full of books with titles like It's His Fault *and* So You Married An Asshole. *And the happily-ever-after Hallmark channel had been abandoned in favor of the all-men-are-bastards Lifetime Network.*

The girl sat on a swivel stool in the bathroom dreaming of getting her first kiss from Dylan Gorsky as her mother French-braided her hair.

"Will you be home when I get back from the dance?" she asked.

The mother adjusted a strand of her daughter's hair with a bobby pin. "I have an appointment tonight," her mother replied. "I'll try to be home by eleven, but no promises."

The girl knew what "appointment" meant. It meant a client. "Why are you still taking appointments?" she said. "Didn't you say that guy Mark proposed to you?"

"I said he proposed," the mother answered. "I didn't say I accepted."

"Why not?" the girl said. "You said he makes a couple million a year. And that you really like him."

"He does and I do," the mother said. "He's my most reliable source of revenue and my favorite client. Why would I spend three hundred and sixty-five days a year with him for free when I can spend one hour a month with him for sixty thou a year? Why would I want him for a husband when I can have him for a client?"

"Love?" the daughter said. "Lifelong companionship? Sex without a contract?"

The mother put her hands on her daughter's shoulders and swiveled her around so that she could see herself in the bathroom mirror. "Look at your face," the mother said, "and tell me what you see."

"A zit," said the daughter.

"Besides that," said the mother. "I mean look at your face as a whole."

The girl looked. She was pretty sure she had eyes and a nose and a mouth, but all she could see was the zit.

"I really wanted my first kiss to be pimple-free," she said. "Do you think Dylan—"

"Focus," the mother interrupted. "Look at yourself and focus. I'm going to say something now, and I need you to listen carefully, because I'm only going to say this once." She brushed her daughter's hair back. "You're a beautiful girl. Before you know it, you're going to be a beautiful woman. And when a man looks at a beautiful woman, he sees one thing and one thing only. A trophy. So if Dylan wants to kiss you tonight, do it. Go ahead and have your fun. If you two decide to start a relationship, have the time of your life. But if he tells you he loves you, watch out. Before you tell him—or any other man—that you love him back, ask him if he'd love you the same if you were flat-chested or twenty pounds overweight. Ask him if he'd still love you if you were a frizzy-haired, brown-eyed brunette instead of a long-haired, blue-eyed blonde. If he hesitates for even a second, you'll have your answer. He doesn't really love you. You're just a trophy to him and he'll throw you to the curb the minute he gets tired of looking at you."

An hour later, the girl was on the dance floor, swaying in the arms of her strong and lovely young man. As the slow song came to an end, his lips met hers, and they kissed for the first time. He asked her to be his girlfriend, and she said yes. They were destined for true love. She was sure of it.

Then one starry night, the teenage couple were making out in the back seat of a car. They'd been together for six months, and she was convinced they would be together forever.

He pulled her in closer as his hand stroked her hair. "I love you," he said.

It was the first time he'd ever said the words, and she was delirious with joy. And finally on the verge of proving her mother wrong. "Would you love me the same if I was flat-chested?" the girl said, secure that the boy's answer would be yes. "Or if I had brown frizzy hair or was twenty pounds overweight?"

The boyfriend didn't answer. Not right away, at least.

"Yeah," he said after a few moments. "I mean, yeah. Of course. I'll love you forever. I promise. No matter what you look like."

A wave of relief swept over her. He loved her, and he'd love her no matter how much she weighed or what she looked like. He promised.

But she couldn't quite make herself believe him. She couldn't move past the fact that he had to take a moment to picture her twenty pounds overweight before he answered. It was the hesitation her mother had warned her about, and she couldn't let go of it. Maybe her mother was right after all.

The relationship went rapidly downhill after that. The girl still loved the boy, and she was ninety percent sure he genuinely loved her back. But that ten percent of doubt came to define one hundred percent of the relationship. She questioned and tested and doubted the boyfriend until he couldn't take it anymore.

And thus it was that their happily ever after turned into never forever within two months of that first "I love you . . . I mean, yeah. Of course. I'll love you no matter what."

The girl had no idea at the time that her first romance would become the prototype for all her romances to follow. As she moved through college and adulthood, she learned that to love a man was to doubt a man. To hear "I love you" was to hear a silent "but" at the end. No matter how hard she tried, she couldn't make herself believe in the happy endings of her princess DVDs. Her teen and adult years had taught her that Snow White would never have gotten that life-renewing kiss if she'd been entombed without makeup. Prince Charming would have sent Cinderella straight back to the attic if she'd shown up to the ball wearing a dress designed by rats. And Rudolph would have flown off into the snowy sky alone, yelling, "Good luck guiding your own goddamned sleigh tonight, motherfucker!" when he realized Santa was a looksist prick who was only nice when there was something in it for him.

The girl was no longer a girl, and she no longer lived in a castle filled with fairy princesses and Prince Charmings. She was a grown woman who lived in the real world, and in the real world, a man would only love her if she was thin and pretty. She was so convinced of it that, anytime a man told her he loved her, she couldn't make herself believe him. There was no way out of it, no hope for real love, because even if she found it, she'd have no faith in it.

CHAPTER 30

IAN

Clara had just invited me into her most sacred private world, sharing some of her deepest and most traumatic childhood memories. She'd told me about being abandoned by her father before she was even born, and about her mother watching the only man who ever loved her die. She'd told me about husband after husband coming and going, and about father after father loving and leaving. She told me about her fragile first love and her first crushing breakup.

And all I could think in return was: *Were Rudolph and Santa in some kind of relationship I don't want to know about? Is there a second verse that never gets played on the radio?*

"So do you understand why I say it's me who ruins all the relationships?" she said.

"No," I said. "I don't. I mean, I get that your mom burned through a lot of father figures and that you witnessed a lot of unhealthy endings. But I still don't understand what any of that has to do with you ruining relationships. And I really don't understand where Rudolph fits in."

"Where Rudolph fits in is that when Santa sees him for the first time, he comes right out and tells Mr. and Mrs. Donner that they're bad people for producing such an ugly fuck of a son. Rudolph's no different from the fairy princesses girls grow up watching. Have you seen a Disney movie lately? There are princesses of every race and culture and size and shape except one: ugly. Or even average, for that matter. I mean, is it any wonder that some of us grow up so pathologically insecure about our appearances that we think no one will ever love us if we're not beautiful? From the day we're born, women are taught that even Santa—*Santa*—will tell us to piss off if we're not good-looking."

I still wasn't sure I was following. "Rudolph's a boy."

"This isn't about Rudolph!" she said, getting frustrated with my stupidity. "It was just an analogy! God, I'm sorry I ever mentioned him. The point is, American folklore teaches girls the same thing my mother spent eighteen years teaching me: the only thing a man will ever love us for is our appearance. But then you get this other lesson, which is that if a man only loves you for your appearance, he doesn't really love you. And you know what? I believed both lessons. Completely. It was a perfect catch 22."

At last, I was starting to understand what she was trying to tell me. I was also finally starting to understand a question from an eleventh-grade English test that I'd gotten zero out of ten points for.

In a hundred words or less, define a catch 22 and provide an example.

Original answer, courtesy of Ian Dunning, sixteen: *A catch 22 is a fish found off the coast of Nova Scotia. An example is a carp.*

Actual answer, courtesy of Clara Zapata, late twenties: *A catch 22 is a dilemma in which two pieces of logic that are mutually dependent upon one another also contradict each other. An example is a woman who believes that the only thing a man could love her for is her looks, while also believing that if a man only loves her for her looks, he doesn't really love her.*

"I think I get it," I said.

"Really?" she said. "You're not just saying that so I won't drag Herbie and Yukon into the conversation?"

"No," I said. "Really. I understand."

She picked at her fingernail, seeming deep in thought. "When I look back now at Jack and Braden and Will, I can see that they were good guys who actually loved me. But I scared them away with my own stupid insecurity."

The more she talked, the better I understood. I understood so well it hurt. Clara Zapata was the female Ian Dunning. Looks were to her what money was to me: the only thing anyone would ever love us for. It was about the most depressing moment of my adult life.

"Do you want to hear something funny?" she said.

"Sure," I said. "I could really use a good laugh right about now."

"Well, too bad," she said. "Because it's not funny. It's actually kind of pathetic."

"Lay it on me anyway."

She continued picking at her fingernail. "At the bar last night, when I was talking to my mother about Tyler dumping me, she said there were only two kinds of men. Rich bastards and poor bastards. She said neither of them would ever give a shit about anything other than my appearance, so I may as well go for the rich bastard."

I could barely believe my ears. "Those were the actual words she used? There are two kinds of men, rich bastards and poor bastards?"

"I was pretty drunk, but yeah, I believe those were the exact words."

"Holy crap," I said.

"What?"

"While you were at Paulie's talking to your mother about men, I was at Geppetto's talking to my father about women. You're not going to believe this."

CHAPTER 31

CLARA

I tried to imagine what could possibly be more unbelievable than the events of my day thus far. There wasn't anything.

"Try me," I said.

"My dad and I get together the first Friday of every month," he began. "That's why we were at the bar last night. There was this hot redhead with obvious breasts implants and he was trying to convince me to talk to her. I told him I preferred a woman with a personality to a woman stuffed with silicon, and his response was that there were only two kinds of women. Pretty bitches and ugly bitches. He said both of them would be more interested in the divorce settlement than the marriage, so I should just go for the hotties."

I was momentarily speechless. There are coincidences and then there are coincidences. And this coincidence was almost cosmic in scope. "Are you serious? That's what he said?"

"That's what he said. While you were in the bar listening to your mother tell you that all men are bastards who only want you for your looks, I was in a bar five doors down listening to my father tell me all women are bitches who only want me for my money."

I felt oddly connected to Ian at that moment. It was the old *misery loves company* thing. Ian and I were two peas in a pod. A giant, miserable, no-one-really-wants-to-eat-you-you-just-look-nice-on-a-plate pod. Ian was the male version of me. It felt good to be with someone who finally understood. "So it sounds like we both got the same bad advice," I said.

He stared out the window at the long stretch of highway ahead. "I'm not so sure about that."

"But you said it yourself. *You're not going to believe this.* And you were right. What your father said to you and what my mother said to me are almost identical."

"But the thing is, your mother was wrong," he said. "That's the difference. When you look back at your past boyfriends, you know they were the real deal. You know that there were men out there who genuinely loved you. When I look back at Greta and Isla and Megan, I know my father was right. All they ever wanted was money. The three of them combined took up eight years of my life, and not one of them loved me back. And it's not just them. Even my girlfriends from high school. None of them—"

"Bullshit," I said.

"Bullshit?" he repeated.

"Yes," I said. "When I said I was stupid before, you said bullshit. And now I'm returning the favor and giving you my uncensored opinion of your theory that no woman's ever loved you. Here it is. Bullshit."

He looked almost offended that I was suggesting a woman out there might actually love him. "What makes you so sure?" he asked.

"Because it's impossible," I said. "It's inconceivable that no one's ever fallen genuinely in love with you."

"You didn't forget that thing I told you about my father being a billionaire, did you? Trust me, with the kind of money my family has, there are literally thousands of women who are ready and willing to not genuinely fall in love with me."

"I didn't forget about the money," I said. "I'm just not talking about it right now. I'm talking about you. Plain old Ian Dunning, with or without the money."

"There's no Ian Dunning without the money," he said. "Ask anyone. It's my whole fucking identity."

"It's not your identity to me," I said.

I knew I'd struck a chord—I could see it on his face.

"I had no idea who you were," I continued. "And admittedly, we started off on the wrong foot. But the more I got to know you, the better I liked you. I was sad when we got back to the city and I had to leave you. You saw me when I was standing outside your car yelling at you to open up. You saw how happy I was to come running back, right?"

He let his head fall back against the headrest. "I saw," he said. "You were happy to see me. But that was when I was still Ian Dundunderfuck. It was before you knew about the money."

"And now it's after I know about the money, and I still like you for you, don't I?"

"Give it some time to sink in," he said. "Once you picture all those zeros in your head, you won't be able to see past them. It'll overwhelm your entire fucking soul. It'll change you and it will change the way you see me, just like it does with everyone else. You'll see."

Man, this guy was determined to believe he was unlovable. "You get that my current poverty isn't hereditary, right? Between the alimony and the freelance earnings, my mom brings in something like half a mill a year. She could retire tomorrow and live more than comfortably for the rest of her life. And believe me, she'd be more than happy to share some of that money with me if I was willing to take it. But I'm not. I haven't accepted a red cent from her since I finished my undergrad. But the fact is, eventually I'm going to inherit everything, so I don't need your money or anyone else's. So, sorry, Ian, you have nothing to offer me on the financial front. I like you for your personality and I couldn't care less about your father's stupid money. Suck on it."

He sat silently, his elbow on the windowsill, his thumb and forefingers massaging his forehead. "I want to believe that, Clara," he said. "I want to believe it more than you could possibly under—"

"Pull off," I said abruptly, pointing to the exit sign just ahead.

"The sign back there said rest area five miles. Can you wait a little longer?"

"No, get off here."

Without questioning me further, he pulled off. At the end of the off-ramp were two signs. The one pointing left said "Downtown" and the one pointing right said "Dead End—No Services."

"Turn right," I said.

"Why right?" he said as he made the turn. "There won't be a bathroom."

"Believe it or not, I don't have to pee." We drove about a half mile further when I saw a ditch on the side of the road. "Right there," I said, pointing. "Pull over."

He veered into the ditch and turned off the car.

"OK, we're pulled over," he said. "Do you mind if I ask why?"

"I want to talk."

"About?"

"You," I said. "I want you to make me understand why you think you're so damned unlovable."

"No, you don't," he said.

"Yeah, I do."

"Fine," he said. "But trust me, you're going to be sorry you asked."

"That's for me to decide," I said. "Spill it."

CHAPTER 32

IAN

In a time that felt like a thousand years ago, in a land that now seemed a million miles away, there was a thirteen-year-old boy who lived in a little red house in a tiny New York town. His mother was a teacher at a school called The St. Ignatius Academy for the Deaf and his father was a rising star in a world known as "finance." The boy himself aspired to be a rising star in a world known as "girls," but was having difficulty getting past the part known as "Hello."

But the boy had a plan. It was the last day of seventh grade, and summer vacation started in four short hours. But more importantly, the first football practice of his life was just two short weeks away. The coach was Mr. Markle, the father of Sabrina Markle. She wasn't the prettiest girl in school, nor the smartest or funniest. In fact, none of the other boys in school seemed to even know she existed. But she was all the boy could think about, and one day when he'd looked over the pages of his history textbook to take a peek at her, he had found her already peeking at him. He'd lain awake until four a.m. that night, delirious with the certainty that he was on the verge of getting his first real live-action girlfriend.

The following day, without his mother's permission, he signed himself up for the football team, his head filled with visions of himself yelling "14, 25, 36 hut" as Sabrina eagerly cheered him on from the sidelines. He wasn't entirely sure he'd be appointed quarterback, what with him never having thrown an actual football or watched an actual game, but he was tall for his age, so surely he'd be assigned to a position of stature. Wide receiver perhaps? Offensive tackle maybe? Goalie?

As it turned out, he would never know, because when he came home that last day of seventh grade, four packed suitcases were waiting for him in the entryway. Before he had a chance to ask his mother what was going on, he saw a limo pulling up in front of his house.

His father's driver, Reggie, was walking across the lawn. The boy immediately ran to the front door and locked it.

Behind him, he heard his mother's footsteps coming down the stairs.

"Let me explain," said his mother.

"You said I didn't have to go to Dad's until August!" the boy cried. "Why is Reggie here?"

"There's been a change of plans," the mother said. Her facial expression was comforting, almost pitying, and he knew she was about to deliver bad news. Putting an arm around her son's shoulder, she led him to the living room, where she sat down on the couch and gestured for him to sit beside her. "I'm sorry I didn't tell you sooner," she said, "but I knew how upset you'd be, so I kept putting it off and putting it off and then suddenly I woke up and it was today . . ."

She trailed off. The boy had no idea what she was talking about, and frankly, he didn't care. As long as one thing was clear.

"I'll be back in time for the first football practice, right?" he asked.

"You're going to have to stay at your dad's until September. But you'll be back in time for the first day of school."

The boy had never been away from home for more than two weeks. And this was supposed to be the most important summer of his life, the one that would lead to his first kiss and being scouted by NFL teams from all over the country. Instead, he was going to be spending it at his neglectful father's obnoxious Manhattan penthouse being inadequately parented by disinterested servants. Was this some kind of cruel joke?

"Mom," the boy protested, his voice cracking, "don't make me go. Please, please, please don't make me go."

"Believe me, I don't want this any more than you do," the mother said. "But it's out of my control. I'm sorry."

"Mom—"

She wrapped her arms around the boy before he could utter another word. "You'll be back in time for school," she said. "The summer will be over before you know it."

"Why do I have to go?" the boy said, now full-out bawling.

She didn't answer, just continued hugging him, rocking him in her arms like a four year old until he was all cried out. "We'll be together soon," the mother said. "I promise."

It was the longest, most miserable two months of my life. The New York City summer was hot and disgusting and I wasn't allowed to go anywhere by myself, not even the park. I had a dedicated nanny, but believe me, she was no Mary Poppins. She was eighty years old if she was a day, and the only song she ever sang was some tribute to Charles McCarthy in A-minor.

Every Tuesday and Friday at around nine p.m., my father would pop his head in my bedroom door and say, "How's it going, son?" I would say, "Okay." He would say, "Glad to hear it." And then our biweekly father-son bonding ritual was mercifully over, not to be suffered again for three or four more days. But all that—the absent father, the ever-present helicopter nanny, the total lack of freedom—all that was bearable. Boring, embarrassing, and frustrating, but bearable.

What I couldn't bear was the loneliness. I missed my friends. I missed my would-be first girlfriend. I missed my bedroom, and I missed being able to ride my bike down the block without a bodyguard. But mostly, I missed my mom. She was the antithesis of Dad. When she asked how I was doing, she actually wanted to hear details. There was no limit to how long she could sit at the kitchen table and listen to me rattle on about school and bikes and baseball and what my plans were for next Halloween.

In short, my thirteenth summer was the summer I realized I had it good. That was the summer when I finally understood why my mom chose to live in a fifteen-hundred-square-foot house in small town America when her portion of the divorce settlement could have easily bought her a million-dollar McMansion in Snobsville, USA. It was because she knew something that I was just beginning to understand: less is more. When it comes to the important things, anyway. My dad had anything and everything money could buy. Or should I say, anyone and everyone money could buy. He surrounded himself with obsequious employees and adoring lady friends, not a single one of whom could actually stand him. As far as I could tell, there were only three people on earth who had ever actually loved my father—his mom, my mom, and me. But he'd alienated his own mother to the point where she couldn't stand him, dumped his wife the minute his net worth hit ten million, and spoke a sum total of about three hundred words a year to his son. He'd thrown away everything truly worth having, all in service of his voracious ego.

That whole summer, I longed to get back to less. I didn't want any more behind-home-plate seats at Yankee Stadium. I just wanted to play catch in the middle of the street with my buddies. I didn't want any more hundred-dollar entrees at restaurants whose names I couldn't pronounce. I just wanted to barbeque hotdogs in the backyard and then feed them to the neighbor's dog through the chain-link fence. But mostly, I didn't want to listen to any more paid servants telling me what a smart and handsome boy I was. I just wanted to sit on the couch with my mom on a Friday night and eat gummy worms and watch *SpongeBob* and then make her promise not to tell anyone that my favorite thing to do on a Friday night was sit on the couch with my mom eating gummy worms and watching *SpongeBob.*

I wanted to get back to less. But less was in a little red house on a cul-de-sac hundreds of miles away, and for reasons no one would explain, my mother was only calling once a week. And at completely random and unpredictable times. Seven o'clock on a Sunday morning. Then Friday night at nine. And even then, our calls only lasted about five minutes. And most of that time was just me begging her to come get me, and her replying, *Soon, Ian, soon.*

But soon never came.

It was a Tuesday in late August at about one o'clock in the morning when I felt a hand shaking my shoulder.

"Ian, wake up, we have to leave right now."

I rolled over onto my back, squinting. "Dad?" It was the first time he'd ever stepped foot into my palatial bedroom. "What's going on?"

"Just hurry up and get dressed. We're leaving in five minutes."

Sitting up, I rubbed my sleepy eyes. "Leaving for where?"

"I'll explain in the car. Hurry, we don't have much time."

Five minutes later, Reggie was pulling up in the Mercedes. When he got out of the car, I presumed he was going to open the door for me. But instead, he hurriedly tossed the keys to my father, who took the driver's seat.

Something was wrong. My father never drove himself anywhere. But as he cruised up the Henry Hudson Parkway at an unholy speed, I finally woke up enough to start processing other weirdnesses. Dad was wearing a pair of pajama pants, a T-shirt, and sneakers. His lower lip was quivering, his hands trembling on the wheel. For my all-about-image father to risk being seen driving his own car in pajamas, his perfect hair uncombed and his perfect feet un-Ferragamoed, it had to be really, really bad.

My first thought was that we were on the run. Every time my disgusted grandmother visited Dad's penthouse, the first words out of her mouth were "It's just a matter of time until they come and get you," so I thought the FBI or IRS or some other scary three-letter federal agency had finally caught on to whatever Dad had done to make himself so rich. I truly believed that the SEC was swarming the front of his building with guns drawn saying, "Daniel Dunning, come out with your hands up!"

Yes, I thought Alan Greenspan had a gun.

I concluded that we were headed for Canada and that Mom, unjustly implicated in Dad's crimes by virtue of association, would be waiting for us on the other side of the Nova Scotia border, the Rocky Mountain Spotted Police waiting to escort us to safe asylum on horseback. Again, I was young. Not exactly an expert on the Canadian legal system or provincial geography.

The point is, I wasn't scared anymore. We were on our way to Mom, and that meant everything was going to be alright. I hadn't had a decent night's rest in two months, but suddenly, I felt very peaceful. And sleepy. I closed my eyes. I must have drifted off instantly, because in what seemed like the very next moment, I was opening them again.

The sun was just beginning to rise. I looked at the dashboard clock. It was six. We were driving down a street in my neighborhood. But we were headed in the opposite direction of my house.

"It's back the other way," I said to Dad, forgetting all about my Canadian escape theory. "You should be driving toward Dawson's Mill Road."

He said nothing. Then, without hitting his blinker, he turned into a parking lot. It was then that I saw the sign: Rosendale Methodist Hospital.

In retrospect, I should have put the pieces of that summer's puzzle together sooner. But it wasn't until I saw the hospital sign that it all became clear. Why I was sent away for two months. Why I was never allowed to call Mom. Why Mom only stayed on the phone for five minutes at a time when she called me. Why Dad, who hadn't displayed a palpable emotion in about ten years, was on the verge of tears.

Holding my hand, Dad walked me to the information desk. "We're here to see Cassandra Dunning," he said, wiping his upper lip and sniffling.

The woman there seemed to be expecting us. "Are you her husband and son?"

"Yes, we're her family," Dad said. It was the only time I ever heard him refer to the three of us as a family.

"Room 336," she said. "I'll let them know you're on your way up."

A few moments later, the elevator doors were opening and I was looking at a sign that said "Oncology" with an arrow pointing left. Unfortunately for me, I wasn't so young that I didn't know what that meant. I had learned it in health class just that year. It meant cancer.

We headed toward Room 336.

Grandma—my father's mother—was sitting on a chair outside the door. Her eyes were closed, her head down, her thumb and index finger systematically rubbing her rosary beads as her lips silently mouthed a Hail Mary.

"Mom?" Dad said.

"Daniel," she said, shocked that he'd shown up. Her opinion of my father was not high, and she never forgave him for cheating on my mom. "You came."

I could see my father's lips purse. But to my surprise, he held his tongue.

"Are we allowed in?" he asked.

She nodded. "She's waiting for you."

I took a step toward the door, but Dad put his hand on my chest. "Can you give me a minute alone with your mom, buddy? I promise I'll be quick."

Dad walked into the room, closing the door before I had a chance to peek inside.

I sat down beside my grandmother, who immediately put her arm around me. She was a big fan of delivering old-people wisdom to her only grandchild, and I knew I was about to get a sermon. "You know that you're all hers, right?" she began. "From the second you were born, you were all your mother's. Do you understand that?"

I didn't.

"You look like her," Grandma explained. "You sound like her. Every good thing about you, you get from her. And I've known her since she was twenty years old and I promise you, she's nothing but good things. And all those bad things your father is—you didn't get any of that. You're not greedy. You're not selfish. You care about other people and you've been that way since the day you were born. So no matter what happens, no matter what any bad person tries to teach you or tell you, just remember that you have your mother's heart beating inside you. And that heart will always tell you what to do. Listen to it."

My grandmother's words would eventually become ones I'd never forget, but at the time, all they did was steal away at precious moments with my mother. I had absolutely no interest in listening to Gran talk about good and bad and right and wrong when Mom was just a few feet away, waiting for me.

Breaking out of my grandmother's arms, I barged into my mother's hospital room. But I was no more than two paces in when I saw something I would never forget. My father was sitting in a chair, his head upon my mother's stomach, his arms stretched over her torso. There was a curtain, so all I could see of my mother was her fragile hand stroking my father's hair as he unabashedly wept into her lap and repeated the same words over and over again. "I'm sorry, Cass. I'm sorry. I'm sorry. You're the only one I ever loved. They never meant anything to me. You were the only one. I know that now. You'll always be the only one. I'm sorry."

I didn't know my father was capable of tears. Or grief, or remorse, or any other normal human emotion. But there it was, right before my eyes. My father, crying. My father, saying he was sorry. My father, admitting he was wrong. My father, Daniel Dunning, humbled before the only woman he ever loved, the one and only woman who ever loved him back.

"Dad?"

He gave my mother one long last look, then gave her hand one long last kiss. Then, without a word, he walked to the doorway, wiping his upper lip.

"Are you ready, son?" he said, sniffling.

I was thirteen years old. Until twenty minutes ago, I thought we were all about to run away to Canada and live happily ever after. So no, I was not ready. But I knew this was my last chance. I walked to my mother's bedside.

She was only thirty-seven, but she looked like she'd aged twenty years in the last two months. She had a scarf over her head and her skin was ghost white. Her arms were bony and frail, almost skeletal. If I'd had any doubt before, I was certain now. Mom was dying. And the reason my father had driven to the hospital in the middle of the night was so I could say goodbye.

I sat down on the chair Dad had vacated.

Mom, looking like it was a struggle just to keep her eyes open, reached for my hand. "Hello, my baby."

I held back my impending tears. My mother had been strong for me any and every time I needed her. Now she needed me to be the strong one. I wasn't going to let her down.

"Hi, Mom," I said, my voice steady as I took her hand.

"I'm sorry I didn't tell you, Ian. The doctors thought I would get better. I was supposed to be back home by mid-August. But it didn't work out that way."

"It's okay," I said, hoping she knew I forgave her.

"Have you been having fun at Daddy's this summer?"

Under normal circumstances, I would have told her the truth: that it was the worst summer of my life and I'd never been so unhappy. But Mom always said that nothing made her happier than seeing me happy. So I played the part. For her sake. "Yeah," I said, faking enthusiasm. "We went to a baseball game last week at Yankee Stadium. We sat right behind home plate."

"Wow," she said weakly. "That sounds really exciting. Could you see their faces and everything?"

"Yeah. And Derek Jeter hit a homerun in the third inning."

"Oh my gosh," she said, "that's so exciting. Wait till you tell—"

She stopped, and I could see she had realized her error. She had been on the verge of saying, *Wait till you tell Bobby and Jay*. But I would never have a chance to tell Bobby and Jay. Because I was never going back to my home and my friends and my school and my happy life again.

Feebly, she squeezed my hand. "You're going to be living with Daddy from now on," she said, getting serious. "And things are going to be different. It won't be like back home. People will treat you differently. They'll all want to be your best friend and constantly tell you how wonderful and smart and perfect you are. But you're not going to believe them. You won't like the things they like or want the things they want. You're going to feel like no one really cares about you, and that the only reason everyone's so nice to you is because of Daddy's money. You'll stop trusting people. You'll start to believe that no one will ever really want to love you. But you'll be wrong. Please believe me. You're a wonderful young man and a beautiful soul. You're worth loving, Ian. If you forget everything else I've ever said to you, remember that. You're worth loving."

By the time the boy arrived at his new boarding school in faraway Massachusetts, the summer was gone and a few scattered *leaves were already falling. The next day, before school even started, he met his new guidance counselor.*

"This is for you," the counselor said, sliding a black and white composition notebook across his stately oak desk. "Every night starting tonight, I want you to spend a half hour writing."

"About what?" the boy said, his tone cynical.

"About your mother," the counselor said. "Everything you remember about her, from your very first memory to your last."

The boy slid the journal back across the counselor's desk. He was mad at the world and everyone in it, and had no interest in the clueless counselor's meaningless guidance.

The counselor gently slid the notebook back. "I can't make you write anything," he said to the boy. "But I'm going to ask you to choose to. Memories are fragile and you'll be surprised how quickly they slip away. Writing them down while they're fresh will keep them safe. You'll be glad you did it someday. I promise."

That night, the boy sat on his bed with the composition book on his lap, reading the words he'd written thus far.

Mom died three weeks ago. My school counselor gave me this notebook and said I should write down all my memories of her before I forget them. I told him I didn't want to, but he says I don't ever have to show it to anyone else and I'll be glad when I'm older.

Just writing the words made the boy angry. He hated everyone on earth for daring to exist in a world where his mother did not, and was sorely tempted to find a match and burn the notebook in a garbage can. But just as he was imagining lighting a match, a forgotten memory suddenly sprung into his mind. It was his mother, lighting eight candles on a birthday cake that was supposed to be shaped like a baseball diamond but looked more like an umbrella. She'd baked and decorated it herself, and they were both laughing so hard at the sight of it that they couldn't extinguish the candles no matter how hard they blew.

Smiling, the boy decided to write the memory down lest he forget it again, this time forever. Then he decided to write down one more memory, this one from when he was three. His mother was sitting across from him at a picnic table, cutting a hotdog into bitesize pieces with a plastic knife and then squirting ketchup into a little cup for him to dip it in. That was it, the entire memory. His mother cutting a hotdog and putting ketchup into a cup. The entry took up two whole lines.

He looked at the clock. The night was young and he had nothing better to do, so he decided to write about the time when he was five and his mother put a gold star sticker on the end of his nose for being a good boy and putting away his own toys. Technically it was just a dumb little sticker, but it felt like an Olympic gold medal. He'd never been so proud.

There was still plenty of room left on the page, so he wrote out the lyrics to "You Are My Sunshine." Then he remembered the time when he was twelve and got knocked over by a wave at Long Beach Island. His mother ran into the water to rescue him in front of about a hundred teenage girls. He was told that he would someday look back on the incident and laugh. He doubted it, but he decided to record the memory anyway, just in case.

By the end of the boy's first night of writing, his counselor was officially the only adult on earth he trusted, and the black-and-white composition book had become his new best friend. He continued writing, night after night, for the entire school year, religiously chronicling every single memory of his mother. As the school year drew to a close and the notebook approached capacity, he started writing in smaller and smaller script so that everything would fit. By the time he got to the last page, he practically needed a magnifying glass to read his own handwriting. But he did it. He fit every memory he had into a single fifty-cent composition notebook. And he used every last inch of white space. In the lower right-hand corner of the back inside cover was his very last memory of his mother, the last words she had ever spoken to him.

You're worth loving.

CHAPTER 33

CLARA

By the end of the story, the trees on the side of the road were casting long shadows over the car. Ian and I were both on our sides in our reclined seats, our heads resting on our hands. Though Ian had been facing me the whole time, he'd barely looked at me once. He had been lost in the memory, telling his story more to himself than to me.

"You're worth loving?" I said. "Those were the last words your mother said to you?"

I expected him to look away, the way he tended to when the conversation got personal. But this time he did not. He looked directly into my eyes and nodded.

I wanted to touch his face. Even if just for a moment. I wanted to reach over, lay my palm on his cheek and run my fingertips down to his chin. And then maybe lean over the console and kiss him. Just for a moment.

But despite his soft expression and the way he was gazing into my eyes, I had no real reason to believe that he was feeling the same way I was. He was just having a moment of vulnerability. And the last thing I wanted to do was take advantage of it.

I stuck to the topic at hand. "Is that why you reacted so strongly when we were talking about Greta? Because I told you that you were worth loving?"

"Yeah," he said. "But it wasn't just that. It was earlier, too. When we were at my house."

I was pretty sure I hadn't said anything about his lovability at his house. If anything, I'd made it pretty clear I didn't want to be within a hundred miles of him.

"Really?" I said. "Because if I recall correctly, I quite literally started running in the other direction when you told me you wanted me to drive you back to the city. I don't think I was making either of us seem particularly lovable at that moment."

He smiled bittersweetly. "It was before then," he said. "When I was in the shed."

"Looking for your keys?"

He nodded. "That notebook I was just telling you about? The one my counselor gave me to write down all my memories? I lost it twelve years ago. I thought it was gone forever. But when I went to the shed to find my spare key, I accidently knocked over a shelf full of boxes. And all of a sudden, there it was, in a box that split open. After all these years, just sitting there waiting for me."

"Is that why you were in the shed for such a long time?" I asked. "Because you were reading your journal?"

"I only read the first paragraph. I wanted to skip straight to the end and read those last words. But I couldn't. I couldn't bring myself to do it."

"Why not?"

"Because I didn't know if I could handle it."

"But it's not like you'd forgotten what she said. How could reading the words on paper be different than hearing them in your head?"

He rolled onto his back and stared up at the car's ceiling. "It's hard to explain. When I was in high school, I was constantly rereading it. I was so lonely that first year at boarding school, you know? Everything I knew was gone. Not just my mother. My home, my school, my friends. But when I was writing my memories, it felt like my mom was there with me. Like it was our book and we were writing it together. And every time I would reread it, even years later, I felt as close to her as I did then. It was like she was there with me again and I was hearing her words in her voice."

"But isn't that something you'd want?" I said. "To hear your mother's voice again?"

He thought it over for a few moments. "If you'd asked me that when I was twenty years old, I would have said yes in a heartbeat. I was still young. I still believed everything she'd ever said to me." He rolled back onto his side to face me. "But it's been seventeen years. Seventeen years, and I'm still waiting for it to be true. I just don't know if I can handle hearing her voice in my head telling me I'm worth loving and realizing that I just don't believe her anymore."

It's funny the way a person's face changes the more intimately you get to know them—how a mean or selfish person becomes less and less attractive and a good and kind person grows more and more beautiful. It's like you stop seeing a face and start seeing a soul. What's on the inside becomes reflected on the outside. And at that moment, with his eyes looking into mine and his soul laid bare, no man had ever looked so lovely as Ian Dunning. He was a good person with a loving and lonely heart. When I first laid eyes on him this morning, I thought he wasn't bad looking. Now he was the most handsome man I'd ever seen.

I touched his cheek with my fingertips. His unblinking eyes were fixed on mine. When I laid my full hand against his skin, he turned his face so that his lips could brush against my palm. Just that tiny little touch of his lips sent a surge of energy through me. I wanted him, body and mind and skin and soul. Almost without realizing it, I leaned over the console, slid my hand around the back of his head, and pulled him toward me. In response, he cupped my head and pulled me toward him. And then he kissed me. And it was no ordinary kiss. It was the kind of kiss I thought only existed in books. Instant fire, all-consuming. I had to have him.

And he was clearly burning with the exact same fire. Hands suddenly at my sides, he grabbed my waist and pulled me over the console. Two seconds later, my whole upper body was draped over his. His warm hands caressed the bare skin of my back beneath my T-shirt, and my hands pulled his shirt out of his waistband. I ran my fingers up to his chest. He was hard, well-built.

I began manically unbuttoning his shirt, and a moment later I was pushing it off his shoulders. When he raised the seat back into sitting position, I straddled his hips. We were now upright in the driver's seat, engaged in what could only be described as a passionate make-out.

As I ran my fingers through his hair, his warm hands crawled up my stomach and over my bra. I sighed. He moaned. I pulled my shirt over my head as he unhooked my bra strap. And there we sat, skin to skin, his hand squeezing my breast as his lips crept down my neck toward my cleavage. I unbuttoned the top button of his pants and pulled down his zipper.

It was at that moment that we heard a knock on the window. Ian's hand on my bare breast, my fingers on his zipper, we turned our heads toward the sound.

Outside our window was a very old man in a very blue uniform. He was holding up a flashlight even though it wasn't dark, and looking at Ian. He did not look happy. He then glanced over at me. Okay, now he looked happy.

"All right, you two," he said, holding his badge against the window. "Party's over. Put your clothes on and step out of the car."

CHAPTER 34

IAN

Just when I thought our adventures for the day were through.

With great reluctance, I let go of Clara's warm breast. It wasn't easy. I hadn't had a woman in eight months, and Clara was no ordinary woman. It goes without saying that I'd sprouted another hard-on the second her fingers touched my cheek.

While Clara politely turned to discreetly slip back into her bra and shirt, I rolled down the window and smiled at the old man.

"Is there some kind of problem, Officer Walsh?" I said, reading his name off his shirt. Technically I knew that getting a near-hand job from a topless woman on the side of a public thoroughfare counted as "some kind of a problem." On a legal basis, at least. On a personal basis, I obviously didn't have an issue with it. But instinct told me to take my cue from every movie and TV show I'd ever seen and deliver the standard line, complete with a polite smile and, if appropriate, a friendly bribe.

"The problem is a Class B misdemeanor," Officer Walsh said. "Public indecency. Punishable by up to six months in prison or a thousand-dollar fine. For each of you. Get out of the car. Now."

I rolled up the window. "I'll get us out of this," I whispered to Clara as I buttoned up my shirt. "Just play nice."

"Trust me," Clara whispered as she combed out her hair with her fingers. "My mother made sure I know what to do in the extremely likely event of a sex-related arrest. My entire life has been leading up to this moment."

God, I hoped I wasn't understanding her correctly. "You're going to have sex with him?"

"Oh, gross!" she said. "No. I'm going to be a nice old-fashioned girl."

"Did you get a good look at the guy?" I said. "I'm pretty sure *he* was the sheriff during Andy Griffith's rookie year on the force. I don't think there's any way to persuade anyone from his generation that what you were just doing is old-fashioned."

"Men from his generation refer to what I was doing as 'dutiful,'" she said. "You're my fiancé, you had a tough week at work, and I was fulfilling my womanly duties and relieving you of your stress in the best way a good woman knows how. I'm sure Great Great Grandpa here will understand."

There was a bang on the window. "I said move your keisters!"

"Our *what?*" I said.

"Keisters," she explained. "It's Geezer-ese for 'ass.'"

We stepped out of the Santa Fe and followed the officer to the back of his patrol car. He didn't handcuff us, but he did do that weird thing where he put his hand on top of my head so I didn't hit it on the doorframe.

As he started driving us north, presumably to the station, I sat without protest, not speaking until spoken to like the proper boarding-school boy I was. Clara, on the other hand, sprung straight into action.

"So," she said, leaning toward the grate, "have you been a police officer your entire career?"

Officer Walsh did not respond.

"My father didn't join the force until he was twenty-eight," she said. "Just after he finished his tour of duty in Iraq. He retired last year. He wasn't ready yet, but he didn't really have a choice, what with the bullet wound and all."

She was really laying it on thick, and not doing nearly as good a job of it as she apparently thought she was. Walsh wasn't biting.

She sat back and focused her attention on me. "I've been thinking about yellow for the nursery. I know you said we should wait until we find out if it's a boy or a girl, but I just can't wait to start decorating!" She clapped her hands together beneath her chin. "I'm so excited!"

I wasn't biting either. Clara wasn't the only one whose single parent had taught them how to behave. I knew the rules when it came to sex-related crimes and proposals of marriage: Don't say a word until you've talked to a lawyer.

"Any plans for Memorial Day, Officer Walsh?" Clara continued. "Having the kids or grandkids over for dinner?"

Dead silence.

"Ian and I are going to a potluck at the VFW. Special ceremony to honor his late grandfather's memory. I'm bringing my famous cheddar-bacon mashed potatoes."

She turned her attention to me. "They were always Granddad's favorite, weren't they, hon?" she said, wiping away a non-existent tear. "Remember that Christmas after we first had the wheelchair ramp installed? He practically ate the whole bowl of potatoes himself!" Sniff, sniff.

An hour later, we were sitting side by side in a jail cell.

I decided I would be the one to break the prolonged silence. "At least you tried."

"I don't get it," she said. "I did everything my mother told me to do. I played the mashed-potato card and everything."

"Don't worry," I said. "Everything's going to be fine."

She looked over at me. "Why are you so calm? You actually look kind of happy."

I shrugged. "I'm just excited about having a new story to tell at Christmas dinner. My relatives were getting sick of hearing the same public erection tales year after year."

Either she wasn't amused or she didn't hear me. I suspected it was the latter—her expression told me she was very genuinely scared of yet another scandal hitting cyberspace.

"My mother's been on the job for over fifteen years without a single arrest under her belt," she said. "But me? I get three seconds worth of unpaid action and I'm facing a six-month sentence."

"You're not going to jail," I assured her. "You're not even going to get charged or fined. This is all going to disappear. My father will make sure of that."

"He couldn't make the picture of you paying me two bucks disappear," she said. "You said it yourself, once it's out there, there's nothing you can do about it."

"Exactly," I said. "And this isn't out there yet. I called the lawyers over an hour ago and, trust me, this is their top priority. Two hours from now, it will be like my father paid God to turn back time."

She looked relieved. I was glad. I didn't actually feel like talking about prison. I had far more important things on my mind.

"You know," I said, jokingly casting a furtive glance toward the cot on the left wall, "if we really wanted to, it's not too late to turn this into another public erection story."

"That's a joke, right?" she said. But she was smiling, even giggling a little.

"Walsh hasn't made an appearance since he locked us in here." I coyly slid my arm around her shoulder like a teenage boy trying to score at a movie theatre in 1962, then began kissing her neck. "The way I see it, we're going to be alone for at least another hour with no other way to entertain ourselves." I lifted my mouth to her ear. "Unless you brought your harmonica."

She giggled again. "You certainly seem to have gotten your flirt on," she whispered, nuzzling me with her nose. "I like it. What's the deal? Do you have some kind of prison fantasy?"

My lips kissed their way up the side of her neck. "I do now."

And just like that, we were kissing so hard our teeth were practically touching, and she was once again climbing onto my lap. I maneuvered one leg over the bench so that I was sitting astride it. She maneuvered one leg over my hips so she was sitting astride me. My hands on her hips, I pulled her in tight so I could feel her pressed up against my insta-rection. Once again, her fingers unbuttoned, then unzipped, my pants.

"Seriously, Clara?" a voice said.

With my hand glued to her boob and her hand just inserting itself down my pants, we turned our heads toward the woman standing outside the bars of our cell.

Clara stood up and walked toward the cell door. "Mom?"

CHAPTER 35

Clara

"It's not what it looks like," I told my mother for the second time in one day.

"Really?" she said. "Because you said the same thing this afternoon when I saw a picture of you accepting two dollars through a car window. Then an hour ago, I get a call saying my daughter's been arrested for having sex in a ditch, and then when I drive all the way here at a hundred miles an hour to fuck the arresting officer, I walk in to find you giving a hand job in a prison cell."

"We weren't having sex in a ditch, okay?" I said. "We were just making out in the car. Which, yes, happened to be in a ditch."

"Just let me have this one," Mom said, looking smug. "You've been getting on my case about my career since you were fifteen years old and now *you're* in a cell giving your fellow prisoner a hand job. This time I get to be the morally superior one."

"I wasn't giving him a hand job," I said. "Although trust me, it's not for lack of trying."

"An attempted hand job with a guy you just met," Mom said, milking her victory down to the last possible drop. "Interesting. What's that thing you always say about nurturing a relationship and taking it slow?"

"Yes, it's true that in chronological time, Ian and I have only known each other for ten hours. But in terms of what we've been through together, we've been married for about thirty years. So actually, what you just saw was way overdue."

Mom leaned in closer to the prison bars. "The way I see it, you need me more than I need you right now, so why don't you just throw in the towel and hand me my victory?"

"Fine, Mom," I said. "You win. Are you happy? I'm finally following in your footsteps."

She reached through the bars and squeezed my cheeks. "I've never been so proud." Her victory achieved, she let go of my cheeks and crossed her arms in thinking position. "So, now that we've agreed that I win, let's come up with a new game plan."

"A new game plan for what?" I said.

She thumbed toward the hallway behind her. "No way in hell am I blowing that guy in the squad room," she said. "He looks like an escapee from a box of Raisin Bran. I've never slept with anyone who fought the Redcoats and I'm not about to start now."

"You don't have to sleep with anyone, Mom," I said. "I really appreciate you driving all the way out here to fellate my way to freedom, but Ian's father is going to take care of everything. We'll both be out of here in less than two hours." I turned to my cellmate. "Right?"

Ian was just staring at us, speechless. I tended to forget that my mother and I didn't exactly have what you'd call a traditional parent-child relationship, and that it was fairly rare to hear a daughter saying, *Thank you for trying to fellate my way to freedom*, in response to a mother saying, *I drove all the way out here to fuck the arresting officer.*

"It's always like this," I assured Ian. "Really, we're best friends. Come here, I'll introduce you."

He walked over and stood beside me. Now that he was seeing my mother up close and personal, he looked even dumber than he had when he first saw her picture. When he continued to just stand there like an idiot without introducing himself, Mom picked up his slack. "Hello, Ian," she said with her most charming smile as she put her hand through the bars for a shake. "I've heard more about you than I ever wanted to know."

Without ungluing his eyes from her face, he accepted her handshake. "You're an extremely beautiful woman," he said.

"I am," Mom said. "Thank you for noticing."

She let go of his hand and turned her head just enough so that he couldn't see her face. "Is he deaf?" she mouthed to me in stealth.

"Yes," I said, annoyed at how distracted he was by my mother in her skintight dress. "But at the moment his biggest issue is stupidity."

"Can you ask him to give us some privacy?"

I looked over to Ian and nodded not-so-subtly at him to step back and give Mom and me a moment. He looked around the one hundred square-foot cell, confused. "Where exactly am I supposed to go?" he said.

Mom answered his question by sticking her pointer fingers in her ears. He obediently returned to the bench and plugged them.

Mom lowered her voice to a barely audible whisper. "You're not really expecting Ian's father to be on your side, are you?"

"I trust Ian," I whispered back. "If he says we're getting out of here, we are."

"Trust him all you want," she said. "But you of all people should know not to trust his father."

"Why do you keep saying that?" I asked, remembering back to a few hours ago when she'd said those exact same words.

"Saying what?"

"That I of all people should know not to trust Daniel Dunning. I'd never even heard of him until today."

"Really?" she said. "The words 'stop this fracking asshole' don't sound familiar to you?"

"What's that got to do with—" I stopped in the middle of my own question, suddenly understanding why it was I should know not to trust Daniel Dunning. "Holy shit," I said. "You mean Daniel Dunning is—"

"The face on the milk carton? Yes, Clara," Mom said. "Ian is the son of the man whose company you and your friends at Eco-Justice are suing for fifty million dollars. If I were you, I wouldn't count on him doing you any favors."

We both looked over at Ian, who was still dutifully sitting with his ears plugged.

Shit on a stick. My mind started racing. There was no way Ian's father could figure out I was a member of Eco-Justice, was there? We had something like fifty thousand members, of whom I was just one.

But I wasn't just any member. I was a team leader and one of the most outspoken voices of the entire organization. Worst of all, I was the one who designed the T-shirt. I was personally responsible for over ten thousand people walking around in public wearing a picture of Daniel Dunning's face under the word "Asshole."

I felt like I was going to cry. "What do I do, Mom? I really like Ian. And he really likes me."

She reached through the bars and stroked my hair. "I don't know, pumpkin," she said. "Even I can't fight off the Daniel Dunnings of this world."

"Do you really think he'll find out it was me?"

"I don't know, Clara," Mom said. "But I'd think that a man with Daniel Dunning's resources could find out anything about anybody if he really wanted to."

I glanced back at Ian. When I held up my pointer finger to indicate that Mom and I needed one more minute, he gave me a really weird-looking double thumbs-up in response.

"You really like him?" Mom said.

"I really do," I said, feeling hopeless.

She then said eight words I never thought I would hear her say. "In that case, I think you should be honest with him."

"Seriously?" I said, flabbergasted. "You're telling me to be honest with a man?"

"Believe it or not, yes. Tell him the truth about your involvement with Eco-Justice. Including the T-shirt. If this turns into a long-term relationship, he's going to find out about it eventually. And if he thinks you deliberately hid it from him, he'll never believe anything you say again. You want him to love and trust you, don't you?"

"Of course I do," I said. "I'm just really surprised to hear you saying you want me to find a man who loves me for my goodness and honesty."

"Did I say that?"

"It certainly sounded that way."

"Well, that's not what I meant," she said. "I just want him to love you because he's rich. Also he stood up to stretch before and it looked like he had a really big dick."

"And that's all you want for me? A rich man with a big dick?"

"What else is there?"

This was why I didn't make a habit of going to Mom for relationship advice. I turned around and gestured to Ian that he could remove his fingers from his ears.

Shaking the stiffness out of his wrists, he walked over to us.

"I don't want you to worry about any of this, Ms. Zapata," he said, his brain evidently having exited his pants and returned to his head. "In an hour from now, it will be like none of this ever happened. And I'm taking care of the bail."

"That's very kind of you, Ian," Mom said, giving him a smile. "I have something for you, too." She reached into her purse and pulled out a set of keys.

"You're breaking us out?" I said.

"They're the keys to the cabin," she said. "You two lay low for a few days. There should be firewood on the porch and extra blankets in the closet if it gets cold. Stop and buy some gas for the genny if you want hot water and electric."

"The cabin?" Ian said, looking at me.

"We have a little place in the Adirondacks," I said, inserting the keys into my pocket. "It's a little rustic, but it's private. We'll be safe there."

It was at that moment that we saw Officer Walsh shuffling toward us with the cell keys in his hand.

"All right," he said, opening the door. "You're good to go."

"That's it?" I said as I stepped out into freedom. "Do we have to sign anything?"

"Nothing to sign," he said. "You were never here."

After stopping for a quick trip to the bathroom, Ian and I walked into the squad room, where we found Mom talking to a young male officer who was feeding our fingerprint cards into a shredder. "It's really too bad your shift just started," Mom was saying to him. "What time do you get off?"

"Mom?" I called, stopping her before she had a chance to thank the strapping young officer in her own special way.

She gave the officer a flirty smirk and waved goodbye.

And that was it. No charges, no fingerprints on file, no paper trail to blackmail us with later.

It was just like Ian said.

It never even happened.

CHAPTER 36

IAN

It turned out that rumors of the wealthy getting special treatment in jail were true. When we stepped outside, the Santa Fe was waiting at the bottom of the steps in front of a sign that said "Parking for Authorized Personnel Only."

I watched Clara and Sara from a distance. They were at the opposite end of the parking lot, engaged in a prolonged mother-daughter embrace.

I was envious. Despite all their bickering and banter, they were obviously very close; whatever had transpired between them in the station was already forgotten. Conversely, the last time my father and I had "bantered" was never, and our "hugs" were the forced embraces that concluded the father-son dinners planned out for us a month in advance by his secretary. And forgiveness? There was no such thing. When I made a mistake, he never let me forget it.

And I knew I was going to be hearing about this latest mistake for many years to come. I looked down at the text that had come through while Clara and I were still in lockup.

Call me as soon as you get this, Dummy.

Dummy. Dad had come up with a variety of pet names for me over the years. When I was a little boy, it was "Dunderhead." *You can't score a goal if you don't kick the ball, Dunderhead.* In my adolescent years, I was upgraded to "Einstein." *The milk goes in the refrigerator, not the pantry, Einstein.* By the time I was seventeen, I was beginning to suspect he'd snuck out in the middle of the night and had my name legally changed to Jesus H. Christ. *Jesus H. Christ, do I even want to know how you managed to have an accident in the car wash?*

By college, he'd grown tired of having to come up with a new synonym for stupid every year, so he downgraded me to plain old "Dummy." It had been my nickname ever since.

Just as I was about to call him and let him have at me, my phone rang. I let it ring five times before I finally picked up.

"Hey, Dad," I said, not looking forward to our oncoming conversation.

He didn't waste a minute. "Remember that time at the country club banquet when Peter Middlebury said, *If you could take a bath with a celebrity, living or dead, who would you choose*, and you said, *The living one?*"

God, not this again. "I was sixteen years old, Dad," I said, rubbing my temples. "What's your point?"

"My point is that I thought you could never, ever out-stupid that one. But congratulations. You finally did it."

"Whatever Walsh told the lawyers, it wasn't true."

"Explain this to me, Dummy. You can afford to have sex in the presidential suite of the Ritz Carlton. *While* the

President and First Lady politely wait in the hallway for you to finish. So why a hand job in a ditch on the side of the road? Do you have some kind of kinky public sex fantasy? Because if you do, trust me, I get it—"

"I wasn't getting a hand job in a ditch!" I said. "We were in a car and we weren't even—"

"What kind?" Dad interrupted.

"What kind of what?"

"Car."

"Why does it matter?"

"It's a car and you're a man. It matters."

I steeled myself. "A Hyundai Santa Fe."

"Oh my God!" he cried out. In my mind, I pictured him clutching his heart. "It just keeps getting worse. Why would you do this to me, son? Isn't it bad enough that you drive around town in a used Toyota? Do you really have to disgrace the family name by getting a hand job in a Hyundai when the whole world knows you can afford to get a blowjob in a Rolls-Royce? If you really hate me that much, why don't you just suck someone's tits in a Kia and kill me already?"

"Believe it or not, Dad, I don't actually want to be known to the whole world as 'Ian Dunning, who can afford to get a blowjob in a Rolls-Royce.'"

"Is it worse than 'Ian Dunning, who can afford to rent a two-dollar whore'? Because that's what the whole world is calling you now."

"She's not a whore! Stop calling her that!"

"Sorry," he said. "Whatever they call themselves these days. A sex engineer."

"She's a PhD candidate at Columbia. And she happens to be extremely intelligent."

There was a pause at the other end of the line.

"No shit?" Dad finally said, sounding impressed. "Is she good-looking?"

"Yeah, Dad, she's gorgeous," I said. "Big boobs, blond hair and blue eyes. She's everything a loving father could want for his son."

"You say that sarcastically, but you might actually be onto something for once in your life. Educated wives are all the rage these days. Bill Beckett's wife from last year had her master's from Yale, and Larry Wentworth once had one who taught at NYU."

"And I assume they both had big tits?" I said, unimpressed.

"Of course they did," Dad said. "No one's saying brains are a replacement for boobs. They're just a nice complement."

I wasn't sure how much more of this I could take.

"So what's her bra size?" Dad asked.

"I didn't ask." I watched as Sara drove away in Clara's Cougar. "Listen, I've got to go. Clara's coming and I don't want her to hear me talking about her fabulous double Ds."

"Double Ds? Nice. You know what, I can't believe I'm saying this, but it sounds like you might have hit the jackpot. Blond, boobs, brains. The three Bs of love. Oh my God, you know what I just realized? A capital letter B is the shape of two boobs. How could I have never noticed that before?"

"Gotta go, Dad," I said as Clara approached. "Thanks for expunging our criminal records. Bye."

I hit the end button just as Clara came within hearing distance.

"Hey," I said. "You ready to get going?"

"Ready," she said, holding up the cabin keys. "Hope you like rustic."

I climbed into the passenger seat of the Santa Fe and we got back on the road.

But we didn't exactly pick up where we left off—with our hands all over each other. Now the space between us seemed about ten miles wide. Whereas before we had been openly sharing our oldest memories and deepest wounds, we were now filling the air with deafening silence. And Clara, for her part, was staring a little too intently at the road, as if deliberately trying to avoid even peripheral eye contact.

"Hey," I said, reaching over and gently massaging the back of her neck. "Everything okay?"

Without looking at me, she gave a polite smile. "I'm fine. Just a little tired is all."

I didn't believe her for a minute. But I played along. "You want me to drive for a while? I feel fine."

She nodded. "I'm good. But thanks for offering."

I removed my hand from her neck, sensing it was not welcomed there. I was starting to wonder what exactly Sara had said to her when they were alone in the parking lot. Whatever it was, it was responsible for a very sudden and unexpected reversal in Clara's attitude toward me.

I decided to try to get the details without coming straight out and asking. "You and your mom seem pretty close," I said.

"We are," she said. It was her entire answer.

"Did you mean what you said about her being your best friend?"

"Yep," she said. "Always has been."

"You two seem so different, though."

"We are," she said. "But we make it work. Nothing's more important than family, right?"

To some families. Once again, I felt a prick of envy. "I like her," I said. "She's got a lot of personality. She wasn't mad at me, was she?"

She looked over at me like I was nuts. "Of course not. You're the one who got me out of jail. You got me away from the paparazzi. You're my freaking hero. Why would she be mad at you?"

I was about to come straight out and ask her what specifically she and her mom had been talking about in the parking lot, but she abruptly changed the subject.

"Was that your dad you were talking to on the phone?"

"It was," I said.

"Did you thank him for me?"

"I did," I said.

"Did he have anything else to say?"

"About what?"

"About me," she said, her voice cracking just a tiny bit.

"Just the regular," I said. "What's she do, what's she like. That sort of thing. Why do you ask? Is there something you haven't told me?"

I asked it casually, like it was a joke. *Ha ha, what are you, a bank robber or something?* But the fact was, her nervousness made me genuinely wonder if she had something to hide. Maybe she was worried that my dad's lawyers had discovered some deep dark secret from her past. "If you have a rap sheet ten pages long," I half-kidded, "it might be a good idea to tell me now."

"I don't have a rap sheet," she said, giving me a nervous smile. "I guess I'm just worried that your dad will disapprove of me still being a student at twenty-eight. Or something like that."

I breathed a sigh of relief. She didn't have a criminal record. And she needn't worry about my dad. She was blond, she had boobs, and she was breathing. The three Bs of love. All Dad's boxes were checked.

"I told him you were a PhD candidate," I said, without adding, *He thinks your degree will look great with your boobs*. "He was impressed."

She let out a deep, relieved breath.

"Are you sure everything's okay?" I asked.

"Everything's fine," she said. She reached over the console and grabbed my hand, her palm just a little bit sweaty. "I guess I just want him to like me."

I lifted her hand to my lips and gave it a kiss. It was terribly touching to see her so vulnerable. At the same time, her assumption that I had the kind of relationship with my father that she had with her mother was painful. It was clear to me that she and her mother trusted each other and valued one another's opinions. Conversely, if Dad liked and approved of Clara, it would make me assume something was horribly wrong with her.

"Don't worry about what my father or anyone else thinks," I said. "All that matters is what I think. And I think you're perfect." Feeling encouraged, I pushed a little further. "So am I allowed to ask what you and your mom were talking about before that was such a big secret?"

"She was just asking me what the deal was with us," she said. "What our plans were and if I liked you. That kind of thing."

"And what did you say?"

She pulled my hand to her cheek. "I told her I thought you were wonderful," she said. She kissed the palm of my hand. And then kissed it again. "And that I really wanted this to work out."

But even as she was saying the words, she looked sad. I would go so far as to say she looked like she was going to cry. There was more on her mind than my dad not liking her. There was something she wasn't telling me.

CHAPTER 37

Clara

An hour later, Ian sat beside me in the passenger seat, sound asleep. As I approached the dirt road that led to the cabin, I hit the right blinker. Not that there were any other cars around to see it. Even at the height of the summer camping season, it was rare to see another vehicle in this stretch of the Adirondacks. And it was still only May. The chances of running into another car, much less another human being, were almost nonexistent. It was the perfect place to keep Ian safely hidden for a few days.

And there was nothing in the world more important to me than to keep him safe. He'd protected me from Carter and the cameras, all the while knowing that he had been branded a purveyor of two-dollar whores for life. He'd gotten me out of jail and had all record of the incident wiped out of existence. He'd squeezed my hand and comforted me when I expressed my fear that his father wouldn't like me, and assured me that he wanted me and that that was all that mattered.

I wanted to return the favor. For the next few days, I wanted him to feel safe and secure and protected, to know that no matter what came our way or whatever twisted lies hit the papers, he had me there to support and comfort him, to tell him that he needn't worry what anyone else in the world chose to believe. I knew the person he was in his heart, and I was crazy about him. That was all that mattered.

I slowed down to ten miles an hour so that the six bags of supplies we'd picked up at Walmart wouldn't rattle too noisily and wake him from his well-earned nap. I reached over and gently ran my fingers through his hair. I imagined him as a boy of eight or nine, all giggly and excited as he fed the neighbor's dog a hotdog through a chain-link fence, blissfully unaware that in just a few short years, his happy young life would be completely upended. Next, he was eighteen, a handsome young college student excited to come home for winter break and indulge in happy memories of Christmases past, only to break down crying when he realized his book of memories was lost and gone forever. And then I thought of him just eight months ago, waking up one morning and finding his fiancé gone.

I wanted it all to be behind him. And for my part, I wanted to be the woman who knew what she had in Ian Dunning: a man worth loving.

The problem was, it was all a fantasy.

I wished I believed in genies. If I had even one free wish, I'd ask my genie to turn back time, to take me back to the parking lot of the police station so I could unspeak the request I so deeply regretted making to Mom.

Tell me what you know about the Dunnings.

She straight out warned me that I didn't want to hear the answer. She said that if I really liked Ian and wanted to pursue him as a romantic partner, I should get to know him for myself and form my own opinions rather than listen to tabloid rumor and gossip that would bias me against him. And, she stressed, I would most certainly be biased against him once I heard some of the things she had.

She may as well have been dangling a carrot in front of a very hungry horse. I *had* to know. So I'd badgered her until she broke down and told me everything she knew about Ian and Daniel Dunning.

On the business front, Daniel Dunning was a self-made billionaire. He had his greedy, extremely powerful fingers in more pies than anyone could count. On the private front, he was a media whore who loved having his picture taken next to whatever uber-babe was hanging from his arm that week. He was rumored to have at least six mega-homes and traveled everywhere in his own private jet. It went without saying that there was a yacht, on which he held lavish parties in the waters off of Monaco and Malta. Daniel had had five wives and about a hundred infidelity partners. But he had only one son, one future heir.

The billionaire-in-waiting formerly known as Ian Dundunfordsomer was famous for being the polar opposite of his father. He was smart, but in a dorky way. He graduated from Tufts and was a computer whiz, but had nothing of his father's ambition or business acumen. And unlike his father, he shunned public attention.

That part I already knew. What I didn't know, however, was that the hermetic lifestyle designed to keep him out of the spotlight ironically drew him further into it. The gossipmongers had labeled him a man of mystery, and his tabloid-inflicted mystique only made him that much more appealing to the legions of single females out there who would kill to be Mrs. Ian Dunning. He'd been unofficially dubbed New York's most eligible bachelor by dozens of websites and gossip columnists.

I should have told Mom to stop then and there. I should have said that I'd heard enough, that I was going to follow her advice and form my own opinions rather than allow myself to be biased by rumor and gossip.

Instead, I stupidly begged for more.

Mom went on to inform me that Daniel and Ian's relationship was a long, complex, and very well-documented one. Ian's mother had died when he was a young teen, and Daniel had handled his new parental responsibilities by shipping his son away to a distant boarding school for the next five years. Ian made no secret of resenting the hell out of his father for it, and after his first Christmas home from college, didn't visit or speak to his father for another three years.

Once again, that part of the story I knew. What I didn't know was that, after Ian graduated from Tufts, he and his father had gone to extensive counseling together and finally healed the wounds of the past. They were now each other's best friends and closest confidantes. Daniel never made an important business decision without consulting his son, and Ian never made an important life decision without consulting his father. They were frequently seen in public having drinks and dinner, and while they were known to bicker, they never parted ways without a hug and a mutual "I love you." It was something they'd learned in counseling—never say goodbye angry.

Based on what Ian had told me about his childhood, I had assumed he couldn't stand his father. But those stories had ended with him at thirteen. That was almost two decades ago. A lot can change in seventeen years. And hadn't Ian said something earlier about how he and his father got on great, that Daniel was a good father and that I'd like him? And when Ian got arrested, didn't he immediately turn to his father, who in turn instantly dropped everything so he could help his son? Those weren't the actions of two people who hated each other. They were the actions of a father and son in a close and loving relationship.

What my mother told me next only sealed my conviction that the Dunning men had, in fact, made amends. Seven years ago, they had founded the Dunning Family Trust together, a charitable foundation that honored the life and work of Cassandra Dunning. Once every six months, they threw famously lavish charity banquets on the family yacht and raised something like forty million dollars a year in support of early childhood and special education.

That last part of the story—where Ian raised and oversaw the distribution of millions and millions of dollars for a very worthy cause in honor of his long-lost mother—was the only part I liked. It was wonderful. It was beautiful. It was the Ian I thought I knew.

Key word being "thought." Because the Ian my mother had described and the Ian I had come to know were two completely different people. I could picture him raising money for a worthy cause, but not sitting at his morally bankrupt father's side at a hundred-thousand-dollar-a-plate banquet table in the middle of the Mediterranean wearing a tuxedo while delivering stale platitudes to the rich and famous while they drank champagne and sampled caviar.

And as for him being New York's most eligible bachelor? No thanks. I wasn't interested in sharing Ian with one woman, much less all of them. Nor was I interested in living my life in a state of constant suspicion. Ian thus far had done nothing to make me believe he was a womanizer, and historically I was hardly what you'd call the jealous type. But boys will be boys, and I wasn't convinced that even a good man like Ian could resist the amount of sensual temptation that must come his way. His father certainly hadn't resisted. The expression "The apple doesn't fall far from the tree" was slowly but surely creeping into my brain.

Daniel Dunning was not a man of character. He was a misogynist who treated women like ornaments, burned through them like kindling, and lumped them all into buckets of "pretty bitches" and "ugly bitches." On the business front, he floated around the globe in a yacht that had the carbon footprint of a small First World nation, and Eco-Justice had all but incontrovertible evidence that he was buying off politicians so he could frack for oil in the preserved habitat of endangered species. And those were just the business entanglements I knew of. God knows what other questionable professional activities he engaged in. As far as I could tell, Daniel Dunning had not a single redeeming quality.

And his best friend in the world was his only son.

It was almost impossible for me to believe, but after what my mother told me, there was no question it was true. Ian was his father's son. It made me realize how little Ian and I actually knew about one another. Over the course of the last twelve hours, we had been building a splendid romance in a tiny bubble. We'd fought and laughed and told each other childhood stories, all the while safely sheltered inside a four-wheeled piece of tin.

But we couldn't stay in this bubble forever. If we wanted this to become a full-fledged relationship, we had to bring our outside lives into the open. Ian's outside life held absolutely no appeal to me. I had no interest in attending events held on an ocean-poisoning yacht overrun by clueless gazillionaires. I had no desire to be the subject of tabloid fantasies or gawked at by passersby every time I walked down the street. And I sure as shit wasn't going to be rubbing elbows—or asses, as our particular case may be—with anyone even remotely connected to fracking and bribery.

By the same token, I had no reason to believe Ian would be any more interested in my lifestyle than I was in his. With the exception of the gas-guzzling vehicle that was the only car I could afford, my whole life was about ecology and preservation. I was a vegetarian who spent every Saturday morning at the farmer's market. I brought home my groceries in reusable bags and used only eco-friendly cleaning supplies. And I'd personally led multiple bird-rescue expeditions under the sponsorship of an organization whose entire *raison d'être* was to fight people like Daniel Dunning. There was simply no denying it. Ian and I could never survive as a couple in the real world.

But for now, we were still safely in our bubble. And I wasn't ready to pop it yet.

Ian, awakening from his slumber, shifted in the seat. One last time, I ran my fingers through his soft hair.

He rubbed his sleepy eyes and stretched. "How long have I been out?"

"Not long," I said. "Less than an hour."

He raised his seat to the upright position. "Where are we?"

"About ten feet from the cabin," I said as I turned into the driveway.

He looked out at the dense forest that surrounded us. "It's secluded," he said. "Even more secluded than my house."

I thought again about the galas, the dirty dealings, the most-eligible bachelor status. But I also thought about how much I wanted to protect him, how much I wanted to be the one who kept him safe. And it suddenly occurred to me that he didn't yet know how much I knew. And he obviously didn't know everything there was to know about me. Which meant he didn't yet realize how incompatible we were. So maybe I could just pretend I didn't realize it yet, either. I could buy myself a few more days of blissful ignorance, cocooned in the cabin with the Ian I thought I knew.

I reached over and squeezed his hand. "It's just what the doctor ordered," I told him. "You're safe now, Ian."

CHAPTER 38

IAN

You're safe now.

The words repeated themselves over and over in my head as we settled into the cabin. They were better than *I love you*, and right there on the mantle beside *you're worth loving*. But it wasn't so much the words themselves that were affecting me so deeply. It was the woman who spoke them. The reason I was safe wasn't because Clara said so. I was safe because Clara was Clara. She would not deceive me, she would not betray me. I trusted her.

I peeled open an oversized can of Walmart-brand raviolis. I'd never stepped foot inside a Walmart before, and I'd been surprised to find that even a rich fuck like me was not immune to its fabled charms. In addition to buying enough canned and dried food to last a month, Clara and I were now the proud co-owners of three one-thousand-count bottles of expired multivitamins, a twenty-four-ounce tube of rubber cement that could evidently fix anything including an airplane, and a coloring book with three free crayons attached.

So I'd gone a little overboard. So I had three more crayons than I would ever need and might end up dying of a riboflavin overdose. What did I care? I was safe and I was worth loving. The love and protection of a good woman were all I had ever wanted in life, and at the moment, I felt like I had both. Not even twenty-four ounces of rubber cement could hurt me now.

Through the uninsulated log walls, I heard the faucet of the outdoor shower being turned off. Right now, Clara was standing naked under the setting sun in a roofless bathroom, wringing out her long blond hair and drying off her beautiful body with a brand-new four-dollar Walmart towel. I'd taken my shower just before she took hers, and I admit that I'd spent a little longer in there than I had to, hoping I'd hear the stall door creak open and turn around to find Clara standing there naked and beautiful and waiting for me. My physical attraction to her was so intense it was almost unbearable. But it wasn't just because she had a pretty face and a gorgeous, curvaceous body. What I was feeling for Clara was way, way more than lust. It was that magnetic pull you feel when you connect with someone so deeply that—

Crap. I was getting excited again. At this point Clara had seen me in the aroused state multiple times, so it wasn't like I had anything to hide. I just didn't want her to think that I'd spent the last twenty minutes in the kitchen imagining us naked in a shower together even though that was exactly what I had spent the last twenty minutes doing.

I had to focus my mind on something unsexy. I'd spotted a lake in the distance when we were unloading the groceries from the car. I imagined myself paddling out in a rowboat with a fishing rod, sticking a hook through a living fish's eyeball, and then gutting and cleaning it with my bare hands only to find a sack of eggs in its stomach and realize I'd just murdered the mother of two thousand babies for my own gluttonous pleasure.

Wow, that worked fast. It turned out a hard-on was no match for a dead pregnant fish. And just in time, too. As my latest erection subsided, Clara walked through the front door wearing the one-size-fits-all bathrobe I myself had been wearing just twenty minutes ago. It looked better on her than it had on me. Probably because I knew she was naked underneath. Technically, she'd been naked under her clothes all day, but this was different. This time there was a bed less than twenty feet away.

Hooks. Fish eyeballs. Two thousand units of substandard caviar.

Ah, crisis averted. Downward dog achieved.

"Hey," Clara said.

"Hey," I said. "Nice shower?"

"Very nice."

"Felt good to wash off the prison vibes, didn't it?" I said.

"That it did," she said. But her voice lacked enthusiasm.

"Why don't you go ahead and get dressed?" I said. "I'll heat up our dinner."

"Thanks," she said without looking at me. "Just give me a few extra minutes to dry my hair."

Without another word, she walked into the bedroom and closed the door behind her.

Something was wrong. I wasn't imagining it. She was growing distant again. She'd been a little standoffish after she talked to her mother in the police station parking lot, but by the time we were in Walmart debating whether to buy a four-pack of canned spaghetti or sixty-four ounces of garbanzo beans for dinner, she'd warmed up again. I'd awoken in the car an hour later to the feel of her fingers in my hair, and right up until twenty minutes ago, when she'd stepped outside for her shower, she was all smiles. What had changed?

Tyler. That had to be it. He was still on her mind. And why wouldn't he be? The nonstop action of our day had served to keep her distracted from thoughts of the wedding, but now her world was quiet again. There was nothing to keep her mind occupied, so it had returned to thoughts of the man who, until two weeks ago, she had thought she was going to be spending the rest of her life with. This time tomorrow, she was supposed to be dancing at her wedding. At this very moment, she was probably supposed to be at her rehearsal dinner practicing her *'til death do us part*. But instead, she was hiding out in a cabin in the middle of the woods wearing a cardboard bathrobe and getting ready to eat a bowl of canned pasta with a spork.

What I wanted more than anything in the world was to climb into a bed with her and never leave. At the same time, I was beginning to feel a little guilty about the pack of condoms I'd bought while she was in the ladies' room at Walmart. True, we'd been on each other like rabbits earlier in the day, but just because sex was on our minds didn't mean doing it was a good idea. Clara was still recovering from a trauma, and I didn't want to push her.

As the timer on the microwave went off, Clara walked into the living-dining-kitchen wearing a pair of pink and white pajamas. Her long hair was dry and hanging over her shoulders in soft waves. I could tell she was wearing neither a bra nor makeup. She was all natural, and she was positively lovely. And round and soft and desirable.

Time to think of a certain dead fish again. By this point I'd named her Mara. She was a friend and her death was personal. What decent man would think of sex at a time like this?

"Sit down," I said, nodding toward the tiny dining table. "Dinner will be ready in a sec."

I poured the ravioli into two bowls and brought them to the table.

"Bon appétit," I said.

"Cheers," she said, raising her spork.

I took my first sporkful of dinner. And literally gagged. "Oh my God," I said, taking a swig of my milk-related product. "I used to beg my mom to buy this stuff. I thought canned pasta was the best thing in the world, right up there with Oreos. What was wrong with me?"

"If you really can't stand the pasta," she said, "there are some Oreos in the pantry."

"We bought Oreos?" I said.

"No," she said. "They're from last October."

"Maybe I'll just stick to bread. And water. I don't know if I can finish the powdered milk."

"Your first meal after your release from prison is going to be bread and water? Nostalgic for the joint already?"

She was warming up again, smiling and making jokes. But I didn't want to get my hopes up too high. I reminded myself not to expect her to be anything less than an emotional roller coaster between now and Monday morning. But that didn't mean I couldn't at least try to help her keep her mind occupied and her spirits up.

"I was thinking," I said, "maybe we could take a walk around the lake after dinner."

"We might want to wait until tomorrow," she said. "The mosquitos are really bad by the water this time of night."

Okay, one idea down. No problem. I had a few more to go. "Maybe we could just sit on the porch? Watch the moon rise? It's clear out, and I think I saw on my phone that tonight's the full moon."

She sucked in a breath, like I'd just said something taboo. "The full moon's tomorrow," she said, her tone suddenly stiff.

"Wow," I said. "You just happen to know the phases of the moon off the top of your head?"

"No," she said. "I deliberately chose May 6th as my wedding day because of the full moon. I scheduled my and Tyler's first dance as husband and wife to coincide with the moonrise." She poked around in her bowl of pasta with her spork, but she wasn't eating. "It was kind of corny, I guess. At least Tyler thought so. He said I was being a bridezilla." She put down her spork without having taken a single bite. "Anyway, I don't know why I made such a big deal out of it. It's just a dumb dance, right?"

She continued staring down at the dinner she wasn't eating, clearly distracted by thoughts of what might have been.

I had an idea.

While she stared at her food, I covertly pulled my phone out of my pocket, laid it discreetly on my lap under the table, and pulled up my weather app.

Bingo.

"Let's go out to the porch," I said.

She looked up at me. "Yeah, alright. Just let me take care of the dishes first."

"Let's do it now."

"It'll only take five minutes," she said. "I'll be quick."

I walked around to her side of the table and pulled out her chair. "I desperately want to go to the porch with you right now."

She gave me a curious look. "Okay," she finally said. "If it's so important to you, let's go to the porch."

Once outside, she went straight to the double-seater Adirondack chair and sat down. I stood in front of her and scrolled through my phone.

"Aren't you going to sit down?" she said.

I didn't answer, just hit the play button on my iTunes and then inserted my phone into my shirt pocket. As the longest slow song on my playlist began to play, I extended my hand.

"What are you doing?"

"The moonrise is starting right now," I said, thumbing to the darkening night sky. "Not quite full, but close." I extended my hand again. "May I please have this dance?"

She smiled a little smile, not quite giggling, but decidedly coy.

"You're not going to make me extend my hand a third time, are you?" I teased. "My arm's starting to get tired."

She hesitated for just a moment, then stood up and took my hand. I pulled her in close and wrapped one arm around her back. She draped one arm over my shoulder and lay her head upon my chest.

The lyrics kicked in, and we began to sway in slow, lazy circles. She was soft and warm in my arms, and I felt like I could dance with her under the moonlight until the sun came up. I lay my head atop hers, hoping that the reason her body was warming in my arms was because she was falling in love with me, not because she was imagining that the man who was holding her was Tyler. I wanted this moment to be about us, not about him.

But I reminded myself how recent her breakup was. I was ready to fall in love again. I was ready to make love again. Clara was not.

And that was okay. Time heals all wounds, and I could wait however long it took for her to recover from hers. We didn't need to have sex tonight. Or tomorrow night, or next week, or next month. Today was just our beginning. There would only be one first time, and I wanted to do it right. No hesitations, no regrets, no ghosts of fiancés past between us. Just pure unbridled passion between two people in love.

There was no need to rush. If things between Clara and me went the way I hoped they would, we had all the time in the world.

CHAPTER 39

CLARA

It was one of those moments I wished would never end. Only it wasn't a moment. It was close to ten minutes. Ian must have picked the longest song on his playlist, the uncut or extended version or whatever. By the time the song was finished, the moon was high in the sky.

I didn't want to remove my head from its secure resting place on his shoulder. I adored the way his body felt against mine. Strong. Solid. Comforting. I wanted to stay this way forever. I wanted us to be just two lonely people who had met one morning under freakish circumstances, hated each other for a few hours, then started to tolerate each other, then to like each other, and somewhere along the line, started falling in love. I wanted to believe that Ian and I were the only two people in the world, that there were no disparate lifestyles to reconcile or disapproving fathers to worry about. If no one else existed, Ian and I could live out our days in a quiet little house on the water, him in his office coding away, me on the surf taking notes on the feeding habits of sandpipers. Then cuddling on the couch after a hard day's work, and then perhaps sharing a slow dance on the beach before retreating to our shared bed for the night.

But I couldn't force myself to believe any of it, no matter how hard I tried. The fantasy in my head was just that: a fantasy. The reality was that I had birds to rescue and ecosystems to preserve and poverty to wallow in. Ian had galas to attend and yachts to party on and hordes of women to fight off. And that was before he inherited his father's money. God knows what kind of person he'd turn into when he took on the official title of billionaire. He'd said it himself—that kind of money changes you. The allure of wealth is too powerful. It overwhelms the conscience and corrupts the soul. Ian was a kind and ethical man now, but what kind of person would he be in five, ten, fifteen years from now? Certainly not the man I'd come to know, the kind of man I wanted to spend the rest of my life with.

With great reluctance, I lifted my head and looked at the face that had become so beautiful to me. Once again, I wished my genie would swoop in and stop time in its tracks, capturing Ian's soul forever in this moment so that he would always remain the sweet and humble man I'd so suddenly and unexpectedly fallen in love with.

My heart skipped a beat when I realized what I'd just said to myself. Not fall*ing* in love. Fall*en*. Past tense. It was a done deal. I was in love with Ian Dunning.

I reached up and touched his lovely face. "Ian," I began. I hesitated, giving my genie a few more moments to make an appearance and dutifully make the world go away. But she was nowhere to be found. It was time to move forward. "There's something I need to tell you," I said. "Something you might not want to hear."

He placed his hand on the back of my head and pushed it gently back onto his shoulder. "It's okay," he said, stroking my hair. "I know what you're going to say. And I want you to know that I get it. Everything's going to be fine."

I had no idea what he thought I was going to say, but whatever it was, he was wrong. Everything was not going to be fine. It was going to be awful.

I felt like I was lying to him, and I couldn't pretend any longer. I pulled out of his arms. "Let's go inside," I said, taking his hand. "We can sit on the couch and talk about it."

He gave me a little nod and a smile. He didn't look worried. He had no idea what was coming.

We sat down on the couch. I wasn't sure how to start. What I wanted to say and what I had to say were two completely different things. I wanted to say, *You're the best man I ever met.* I wanted to say, *You're my dream come true.* I wanted to say everything I'd ever seen on a cheap candy heart. *B Mine 4ever. Soul M8. Kiss Me.*

But what I said instead was nothing. It was like I had freaking sleep paralysis. I was so scared of facing the end that I couldn't even open my mouth.

Ian solved my problem for me. He took both my hands in his. "It's only been two weeks," he began. "The wedding was supposed to be tomorrow and no one in their right mind would expect you to get over Tyler so quickly. The last thing I want is to rush you into something. I want you to know that I'm fine taking this slow. We can take as much time as we need to do this right and make it work."

"You think this is about Tyler?" I said. "You think I'm still thinking about him?"

"I mean, yeah," he said. "You were just talking about him at dinner. And about the wedding. And you seemed so sad—"

"I wasn't thinking about Tyler," I said. "When you said that thing about the full moon, the wedding popped back into my head for a minute. But I've barely been thinking about Tyler at all."

"You haven't?" he said, looking relieved.

"No," I said. "You're the one I can't stop thinking about."

Now he looked more than relieved. He looked happy. Worse than happy. Hopeful. Which meant that telling him what was really on my mind was going to be that much harder.

I cast my eyes down so I didn't have to look him in the face. "It's true that I can't stop thinking about you," I said. "But it's not what you think. It's not—"

His hands loosened their grip on mine, and I knew he was finally starting to believe me when I told him this wasn't going to be good.

"Just tell me," he said. "Whatever it is, just say it and get it over with."

Keeping my eyes down, I just spit it out. "I haven't been completely honest with you."

He inhaled sharply and I immediately squeezed his hands in reassurance. "Not like Greta and the others," I clarified. "Please, believe me, I don't mean that I lied to you or deliberately deceived you. I just mean that I haven't told you everything. About me. About who I am and the people I associate with and the way I live my life. And you have the right to know."

He remained silent, looking down at our joined hands.

"You're a good person, Ian," I continued. "And you deserve the chance to hear about my beliefs and life choices before you make any decisions." I lifted his hands to my lips and held them there. "You're my dream come true. But when you hear about the things I've done, I have a feeling you're not going to think the same of me."

For another moment—a moment that might be our last—I held my lips to his skin. I wanted to feel him and taste him, to pretend that I believed that today was the first day of the rest of our lives and that Ian's strong hands were mine to hold forever.

But Mom had taught me to be a realist, to look cold hard facts in the eye and accept them for what they were. She had raised me right. I just sometimes wished she hadn't done such a damned fine job of it.

Without another word, I let go of Ian's hands and walked into the bedroom. Opening my duffle bag, I found the "Asshole" shirt, folded right there on top. I brought it into the living room and sat cross-legged on the couch beside Ian.

I placed the shirt in the space between us, then turned my face toward the wall so I wouldn't have to look him in the eyes. "Do you recognize this shirt?" I said.

His response was silence. I kept my eyes averted.

There was a painful, prolonged silence before he finally spoke.

"Oh my God," I finally heard him say. "I can't believe it. I can't believe you just asked me that."

In that moment, all my fears were realized, all my hopes dashed. He was on his father's side. He could never be with someone like me. And I could never be with someone like him.

"I'm sorry, Ian," I said, struggling to control my emotions. "But it's better for both of us that you know the truth. A small part of me wanted to believe you felt the same way I do. But deep in my heart, I knew that—"

"Feel the same way?" he interrupted in disgust. "Are you kidding me? What the hell kind of person do you think I am?"

"I think you're wonderful, Ian," I said, finally mustering up the courage to look him in the eyes again. I grabbed his hands. "Just listen to me, please. I think you're sweet and loving and genuine. That's the kind of person I think you are. You have no idea how much I want to believe you could love me and we could make this work. But you have to understand, this represents everything I believe in. I'm dedicating my whole life to it, and I can't have a relationship with a man who doesn't at least *kind* of feel the same way I do."

He ripped his hands out of mine and stood up. "Let me rephrase my previous question," he said, clearly unimpressed with my pleas. "Forget *what the hell kind of person do you think I am*. What the hell kind of person are *you?*"

My sadness began to morph into anger. "Really?" I said. "Do you really live such a sheltered life that you don't see how important this is? Do you really not understand that this is one of the most critical ethical issues of our generation?"

"No, I don't!" he said. "And if you support it, then *you're* the one with the ethical problem."

"*I* have an ethical problem?"

"To put it mildly."

"We're talking about the future of the whole world here, don't you get that?" I said. I stood up, gloves on and ready to fight. At last, I was starting to see the rich spoiled brat, the clueless billionaire in the ivory tower. "We're talking about giving our children a safe planet to grow up in!"

"Exactly," he said. "Which is precisely why I can't understand how you can stand there and tell me you support raising your future daughters in that kind of world. Or future sons, for that matter."

"Sons or daughters, what does it matter?" I said. "Boys need clean air to breathe and clean water to drink just as much as girls do."

"What do clean air and water have to do with it?"

"Everything!" I said. "What the hell do you think we're talking about here?"

"I don't know," he said, frustrated. "You tell me!"

"I'm talking about this," I said, gesturing to the shirt on the couch. "I said, *Do you recognize this shirt?*"

He looked down at the shirt. For a moment, he was silent. "Do you recognize this shirt?" he repeated, the anger in his voice suddenly evaporating.

"Yes," I said. "Do you recognize this shirt. What did you think I said?"

He turned his glance to me, then back down to the shirt on the couch. Then back to me.

"I thought you said, *Do you want some ISIS merch.*"

It took me a few seconds to process that one. "ISIS merch?"

"That's what I heard."

"What the hell is ISIS merch?"

"I don't know!" he said, gesturing to the folded-up shirt on the couch. "A T-shirt, I guess. A hoodie or beanie. A lunchbox maybe."

"What the hell kind of psycho would send their kindergartner to school with an ISIS lunchbox?"

"The hell if I know!" he said. "I heard you say 'ISIS' followed by the word 'merch.' I didn't even know they had a YouTube channel, much less an online shop. I had to use my imagination and trust me, it wasn't pretty."

I felt my body start to convulse and my knees begin to buckle. I flopped onto the couch, clutching my side. "ISIS merch!" I repeated, suddenly imagining a six-year-old girl in a school uniform skipping to the bus stop with an "I Heart ISIS" lunchbox in her hand. Tears ran down my face as I struggled to breathe through my laughter.

When I finally came up for air, Ian was sitting on the couch again. His elbows were on his knees, his head was in his hands, and his entire body was shaking with laughter.

"Oh my God," he said. "That was worse than when I thought you took stool samples from your customers."

I took a few deep breaths, trying to get myself back to a normal heart rate. "You actually thought I was an ISIS supporter?"

"Yes," he said, his laughter at last beginning to subside. He wiped a tear from his eye. "You were going on and on about the things you've done and the people you associate with and how you were dedicating your whole life to the cause. You sounded so serious. What was I supposed to think?"

Feeling much more lighthearted than before, I grabbed the T-shirt and unfolded it. "I was talking about this," I said, holding it up for him to see in all its rectal glory. "Does it look familiar to you?"

He took the shirt from my hands and looked at it for a moment. "Yeah, I recognize it," he said, tossing it back onto the couch. "What about it?"

It wasn't the reaction I expected. Not even close.

"It doesn't bother you?" I said.

"No," he said, weirdly nonchalant. "Why would it?"

"Because it's a picture of your father with the word 'asshole' above it?"

"Like I said, I've seen it before. You have one, too?"

"I have twenty," I said.

"Got you beat," he said. "I have a hundred. A hundred and ten, actually. For every ten you buy, you get one free."

"That was you?" I said, shocked. "That was our single largest order."

"Really?" Ian said, looking surprised. "No one else bought that many? Not even my grandmother?" He stopped as he at last seemed to grasp what I was telling him. "Wait a minute," he said. "How do you know mine was the largest order?"

"I know because I'm a team leader at Eco-Justice," I said. "We're suing your father's company for fifty million dollars. I'm the one who designed the shirt."

For a moment, he just stared at me in shock. "You designed the shirt?" he said at last.

"Yes," I said, starting to get nervous again. "It was just supposed to be a joke. Really. But then we started getting all these orders—"

Before I could finish, his arms were around me and he was rocking me side to side, showering my head and face with kisses. "Oh my God," he was saying between kisses, "if you weren't the girl of my dreams before."

There in his arms, I felt myself beginning to smile. Then to outright laugh. "You mean you're not mad about this?"

"Of course I'm not mad," he said.

"But I told the whole world your father is an asshole."

"The whole world already knows that," he said, resuming his manic kissing. "You're just the first person to put it on a shirt. Oh my God, you're perfect. I've never been so happy in my whole life!"

CHAPTER 40

IAN

I couldn't stop kissing her. "Thank you!" I said. "Thank you, thank you, thank you!"

She was giggling like a schoolgirl. "Thank you for what?"

"For passing out drunk in my car," I said. "For selling your body on the street and working outside of your species. For peeing on a fire hydrant and raising money for terrorists."

She pulled back. "Peeing on a fire hydrant?"

I pulled her back in. "And for making me finally accept the fact that I need to get a hearing aid." I squeezed her tight. "Thank you."

At last, our joy-induced laughter subsided and our bodies separated. Grasping both her hands in mine, I pressed my forehead against hers. "Did you really think I was going to reject you because of my father?"

"Kind of," she admitted. "My mother told me that after college, you and your dad went to counseling and now you were really close. She said that she read that you never make an important decision without him."

Goddamned public relations team. Fucking tabloids. Between the two of them and their endless lies, they could have cost me my chance with Clara.

"Please," I said, "don't believe everything you read about me. That thing about counseling? It's all bullshit. During my senior year at Tufts, someone published an exposé about how my father was such a prick that even his own son and mother couldn't stand him. His reputation was already at an all-time low, so as damage control, his public relations team arranged for us to meet with a family therapist. My dad showed up for exactly one appointment. But he paid the therapist for the next three years so that he could honestly tell the world that he had regularly scheduled counseling sessions with his son."

"But you *did* work things out, didn't you?" she said. "My mom said that every time you're together, people see you hug each other and say I love you."

"Yeah, that's true," I said. "We learned it in our one and only therapy session. It's a technique called behavioral modification. Hug and say 'I love you' at least once a week, and supposedly one day you'll wake up and it will be true. We've been going through the motions ever since."

Her expression grew sad, almost pitying. "You don't love your own father?"

It was a tough question, one I asked myself on a regular basis. And there was no easy answer. "Yeah, I love him," I said. "And he loves me. We're a family, we can't help it. But it's not like what you have with your mom. The minute I saw you two together, I could tell either one of you would jump in front of a bus for the other. But my dad? Once he made his first ten mill, he turned into a person no one recognized anymore. He'll never love another person as much as he loves money. And that's never going to change."

She still seemed sad. Or worried or something.

"But what about you?" she said. "You're going to inherit everything one day. Aren't you worried that the money will change you the way it changed him?"

"No," I said. "I'm not. Are you?"

She winced. "I mean, you said it yourself. That kind of money eats away at your soul. It's inevitable."

"The inheritance isn't going to change me," I said.

"How can you be sure?"

"Because there's no inheritance."

She pulled back, shocked. "Really?"

"Really," I said. "After Greta, I decided I couldn't take it anymore. I just wanted what everyone else wants. Genuine friends, a family to take care of, a wife who loves me. I'll never be able to have any of that if I'm the billionaire's son. So I traded in my Mercedes for a used Toyota. I sold the condo in the city and moved full time to the house in Connecticut. And about a month ago, I finally bit the bullet and talked to a lawyer about getting out of my father's will."

A perplexed look crossed her face. "You have to consult a lawyer about getting out of a will?" she said. "Can't you just tell your father you don't want the money?"

"It's complicated," I said. "There's an irrevocable trust. There's irrevocable life insurance. And I'm the president of my mother's foundation. When I tell my father I don't want his money, he's going to take it personally. I don't *think* he'll dissolve the trust out of spite, but I wouldn't put it past him. So yeah, I need to figure things out with a lawyer before I talk to my father. I need to make it diplomatic."

She stared up at me, still in utter disbelief. "So that's it?" she said. "You're just going to be a normal average-income guy?"

"No," I said. "I still make three hundred thousand a year on my own and I inherited a few million from my mother. I'll always be well off. But I'll never be a billionaire. Not even close."

I expected her to breathe a sigh of relief, or at least to smile a little. But she did not.

"Can I ask you one last thing?" she said.

"Sure," I said, beginning to get a little worried myself. Now that she knew I was never going to be a billionaire, was she changing her mind?

She rested her forehead against mine again, keeping her eyes cast down. "So if there's not going to be an inheritance, does that mean . . . does that mean you won't be New York's most eligible bachelor anymore?"

I closed my eyes as a relieved—and deeply touched—smile crept across my face. She didn't care about my money. But she did care about having me all to herself.

"I was never New York's most eligible bachelor," I assured her, squeezing her hands in mine. "I was a hot ticket for gold diggers. But trust me, once the news that I've been disinherited gets out, I'll never get another naked selfie from a stranger again. I'm all yours, Clara."

Eyes closed, she smiled as she brought my hands up to her lips. "I'm all yours, Ian."

I don't think I'd ever felt so peaceful, so contented, in my entire life. So this was what trust felt like. A beautiful woman holds your hands and tells you she's all yours, and you believe her. I untangled my fingers from hers and placed them on her cheeks. I wanted her. But more than that, I needed her.

I pulled her face in closer to mine, and kissed her.

CHAPTER 41

CLARA

It wasn't our first kiss. Nor was it our first touch. But it wasn't the same mad-groping, clothes-tearing horniness as earlier. Now it was all slow hands and gentle kisses, sensual fingers and soft lips. I ran my hands across his cheeks and over his mouth, luxuriating in the prickly stubble of his day-old beard, the soft warmth of his open lips. I wanted him, but it was way more than just pure animal lust. He was all mine, and I wanted to be a part of him, to mingle with him until we were so tangled up with one another that I didn't know where his body ended and mine began.

As his mouth worked its way across my face and down my neck, I straddled his lap. We'd been in this same position before, but in the car and jail cell, we'd been separated by bulky fabric. Now Ian was in a pair of sweatpants and I was in a pair of pajamas. With nothing but two thin layers of polyester between us, I could feel the distinct shape and hardness of his erection, and as he rubbed back and forth against me, the silky fabric teased me.

His hands began exploring. As he moved over my hips and down to my thighs, he made a realization. "No panties?" he said, breathless.

He liked it. And I loved that he liked it. "No panties," I said.

He exhaled in stilted breaths. I grabbed his wrists tight, pulling his hands from my hips and placing them at my waist under my pajama top. I wanted his skin on my skin, and he didn't disappoint me. His hands on my breasts were gentle and warm. As he squeezed, I slid my hands under his shirt, letting my open palms slide up over his firm abdomen on their way to his chest.

He let go of my breasts and reached up for the top button of my pajama top. One by one, he began unbuttoning. He took his time, a slow seduction. And a very successful one. With each button he unbuttoned, I grew more eager to feel his bare skin against mine.

When he at last undid the final button, he slipped my top off my shoulders and let it fall to the floor. I pulled his shirt over his head and tossed it aside, then wrapped my arms around his back. Sucking on his neck, I ran my fingertips up his spine, then rested my hands on the curve of his shoulders. As his hands moved down my back, he thrust his hips upward, his chest hair tickling my breasts as his erection poked at me hard. I couldn't remember the last time I'd desired a man so badly, or if I had ever desired a man so badly. Ian was all mine, and I wanted him.

And he wanted me. As his hands reached the small of my back, his lips found their way back to mine. Kissing me, he grabbed my behind. But he was growing more excited, and his eager hands were no longer so gentle. Squeezing me hard, he pushed my whole body up so that his mouth could latch onto one breast. As his fingertips ran down the crease of my behind, I inserted both my hands down the front of his sweatpants, where I found him big and hard and ready for me in his tight boxers. He moaned as I squeezed him. I couldn't wait any longer.

"Ian," I said, "let's go to the bedroom."

He was more than happy to comply. Pulling my legs around his waist, he rose to his feet. Kissing me as he carried me, we passed through the door into the bedroom, and a moment later, he was laying me down on the bed.

He stood beside me, one foot on the floor and one knee between my thighs. The light of the near-full moon was streaming in from the window, and he was beautiful in its soft glow. I flashed back to earlier in the day, when he first told me about the loneliness of his childhood. I remembered how much I wanted to touch his face, how much I wanted to hold him and kiss him. This moment was no different. I wanted to make love to him, but I also just wanted to hold his head in my hands and look at him.

I brought his face to mine and kissed him. As I touched his cheek, he grabbed my pajamas at the waist and pulled down. I returned the favor.

And then there he was, on top of me, both of us naked. I loved the weight of his body on top of mine, the warmth of his skin against my skin. His knees nudged at mine, pushing them outward. I opened up for him, and then a moment later he was in me.

He was deliciously hard as he moved in long, slow strokes. I moved with him in rhythm, grabbing the bars on the headboard so I could push myself harder against him. His strokes quickened, and his sighs told me he could feel me gripping him tighter as my excitement grew. He thrust deep and fast again, then again and again. My hips reflexively jerked up as I reached climax, and he let out a delightful moan as I spasmed against him. A moment later he made one deep, final thrust, then froze in position as he orgasmed.

"Oh my God," he said, panting as he collapsed on top of me.

"Good?" I said through stilted breaths.

He pulled out and rolled onto his back, placing his hand over his heart. "I think a fairy just got its wings."

We both started laughing. I wasn't sure if it was because of his euphemism or just because we were so damned giddy. But I suspected it was more the latter.

Closing my eyes, an image rose to my mind. Ian and I were sitting in the car in standstill traffic. I was in the passenger seat, reading a hand-carved cupcake. His message to me was simple, ordinary, but it captured everything I wanted from him and everything I wanted to give him in return.

I grabbed his hand. "I'm happy, Ian."

His eyes were closed, but he was smiling. He gave my hand a squeeze.

"I'm happy, too, Clara."

One Year Later

Ian

I watched from the kitchen window as Clara sat cross-legged on a blanket about ten feet from the surf, observing the sandpipers scamper back and forth across the wet sand as the pink light of sunset glowed on the horizon. She had a small notebook on her lap, but her pen was tucked behind her ear. She hadn't written anything in about a half hour. I wondered what she was thinking. Perhaps something to the effect of: *Let me in, Ian, it's cold out here.*

No, our relationship hadn't gone so far downhill over the course of the last year that we'd started locking each other out of the house. But it had progressed to the point where she was three months pregnant, and I didn't want her breathing the air in the house until the paint fumes from the nursery had fully dissipated. So when she'd stepped outside three hours ago to go to the mailbox, I pushed the heaviest piece of furniture we owned—a solid oak antique dresser—in front of the door.

So on a purely technical basis, yeah, I guess I did lock her out of the house. But my intentions were good. And her mom was on my side.

"She's going to thank us for this when the baby is born with only one head, right?" I said.

Sara came to the window and stood beside me. "I wouldn't count on it."

"What do you suggest we do?"

"I'm going to tell her it was all your idea and I was against it," she said. She looked over at me. "What's your plan?"

I knew better than to argue. "What do you suggest?"

Sara placed her pointer finger on her bottom lip, looking off into the distance as she pretended to think it over seriously. "Hmm," she said. "What if you told her that you gave her mother gas money for the ride home? I think she'd really like that."

"You think that, do you?"

"I do," she said, holding out one open palm.

I pulled my wallet from my back pocket. "The Zapatatude wins again," I said as I dutifully pulled out a fifty-dollar bill and handed it to her. She promptly rolled it up and inserted it into her cleavage, which is where she kept most of her trophies, including the keys to the brand-new Lexus some guy gave her last week.

"Who'd you get a new car out of, anyway?" I asked.

"I think the better question is, who *haven't* I gotten a new car out of?" she said. "You don't think I spend my own hard-earned money on transportation, do you?"

In terms of badassness, Clara's mother made my father look like a puppy dog. But she was also the world's best hugger, which made up for her multitude of pain-in-the-assities.

Her arms open and waiting for me, I accepted her thirty-second-long bear hug, along with a kiss on the cheek. When she at last let go, she slipped into her high heels and waited patiently as I pushed the two-hundred-pound dresser away from the door.

"Are you really going to tell her it was all my idea?" I said as I opened the door.

"Yes," she said as she stepped onto the porch. "Don't forget to call your father."

"I called him last week."

"Call him again."

Without another word, she closed the door behind her. A moment later, I heard her drive away.

I'd go through the motions of calling my father another day. Not that there was any point. He hadn't returned any of my calls since my lawyer first contacted him about the will. But while he hadn't spoken to me in three months, I was sure he was keeping tabs. Which meant he no doubt knew that Clara and I had run off to Maine and eloped last month. We hadn't told anyone but Sara about the pregnancy yet, but now that Clara was officially in her second trimester, it was only a matter of time before our secret was out. Dad's ego might be bruised over having his money rejected and being denied the opportunity to turn our wedding into his own personal advertising event, but when he found out he was going to be a grandfather, he'd come around. I was sure of it.

But until then, I had other matters to attend to.

Clara was still sitting on the beach watching the sandpipers. Hopefully she would forgive me when I told her we had reservations at her favorite restaurant. I had everything planned out. Alcohol-free dinner, a moonlight walk on the boardwalk, then an overnight at a cozy hotel. Tonight was the anniversary of the night she'd passed out in my car, and I really wanted it to be more memorable than the night she passed out in my car.

Now that our lives had become so peaceful and simple, it was incredible to think back on the series of bizarre events that led to those first twenty-four hours. Clara liked to say it was fate or destiny, but personally I didn't think destiny had that twisted a sense of humor. Besides, our story was much more interesting than anything the gods of love could have come up with. If it had been up to the heavens, we would have met reaching for the same slice of watermelon at a church picnic or something boring like that. Instead, the tale of how we met and fell in love was second in entertainment value only to the story of why we had a framed sanitary napkin on our dining room wall. Yes, my wife had a sense of humor. And it was a good thing, too. At the moment, I was choosing to believe that ten years from now, she'd be telling our kids about that time she was three months pregnant and Daddy locked her out of the house because he was afraid that if she breathed in paint fumes, little Bobby or Suzie would be born with a dorsal fin. *God, that crazy dad of yours. What a character. Such great memories.*

But she'd been out there for three hours now, and it was time to come to her rescue. I grabbed a blanket off the back of the couch, stepped outside, and headed toward the surf.

The sand silencing my footsteps, I snuck up behind her. I grabbed her shoulders, and she jumped.

"God, you scared me," she said, then looked at the blanket draped over my shoulder. "What's that for?" she said, giving me a fake dirty look. "Are you planning on making me sleep out here tonight?"

"It's to keep you warm," I said, sitting down beside her and wrapping the blanket around her shoulders. "The paint fumes are still a little strong."

"How much longer do you plan to keep me locked out of my own house?"

"Another twelve hours or so," I said. "But we can go straight to the restaurant from here."

"The restaurant?" she said.

"I made reservations at Gillian's. Then we're booked for the night at The Surfside." I wrapped my arm around her shoulder and gave her a kiss. "Happy anniversary."

As kisses went, it was a nice one. At any rate, I was pretty sure I was forgiven.

"Happy anniversary," she said, rubbing her nose against mine.

I gestured to the pad of paper in her lap. "What's the notebook for?"

"Baby names," she said.

"Can I see?"

"No."

"It's my baby."

"Or so you choose to believe."

I teasingly wrestled it out of her hands and opened to the first page.

"See any ones you like?" she said.

I read through the boy list. "I kind of like Henry."

"You don't think it's too old sounding?" she said. "I don't want the other kids to tease him."

"I guess it's a little old-fashioned," I said. "But I still like it. Henry Dunning. Has a nice ring to it."

"What about Charles?" she said. "It's a little more youthful."

"Too regal," I said. "Feels pretentious."

She took her pen from behind her ear and crossed out Charles. "What about from the girl list?"

I looked at the list. The first several names were straight out of the classic name catalogue. *Margaret. Elizabeth. Charlotte. Rachael.* About twenty names on, they started getting a little exotic. *Athena. Harley. Zoe. Willow.* From there, I couldn't help but notice a theme developing. *Ariel. Marsha. Shelly. Marina.* A hundred or so names in, and it was clear that I'd left my wife baking in the sun too long. *Surfina. Pebbles. Fruity Pebbles. Sandy. Piper.*

"If our daughter ends up going through life with the name Hightidia," I said, "I guess I'll only have myself to blame."

"I don't know," she said, shrugging. "I actually kind of like the idea of her going around introducing herself as 'Pebbles—Fruity Pebbles.' She'll be Connecticut's own James Bond."

I grabbed the pen from behind her ear and wrote "VETO" in large letters across the entire bottom quarter of the list. Then I scribbled in a suggestion of my own.

"What about this one?" I said, handing her the notebook.

"Mara?" she said.

"An old fish friend of mine," I explained. "You would have liked her. At the moment, you two have a lot in common."

She gave me a cynical look. "Was this the pregnant trout who was supposed to keep us from having sex fourteen hours after we first met?"

"So you remember her."

She held up her pointer finger. "She had one job, Ian. One. Do you really want to name your first-born child after someone so incompetent?"

"I'll have you know that Mara's professional ineptitude is responsible for one of the happiest memories of my life," I said. "I'd be proud to name my child after her."

"And what are you going to tell our daughter when she's seven years old and says, 'Daddy, my teacher told us to write a paragraph about how our parents chose our names.'"

"Fine," I said, grabbing the pen and crossing Mara off the list. "What about Tara or Lara? Or Zara?"

She took the pen from my hand, turned to a fresh page in the notebook, and scribbled down another name. "I've been thinking about this one," she said, handing it over. "What do you think?"

I looked at the name. It was a good one. Perhaps the best so far.

"Cassandra," I said aloud. "It's perfect."

Made in the USA
Monee, IL
03 June 2023